Letters to Santa

SARAH LAMB

ISBN paperback: 978-1-960418-29-6
ISBN large print: 978-1-960418-30-2

Contents

For those who are needing a little extra Christmas cheer this year, I hope you will have it.

Chapter 1

1913, Richmond, Kentucky

"Have a lovely afternoon," Edith Clarkson said from behind the bank's counter. The balding, middle-aged customer nodded curtly and left, tucking the money he'd withdrawn into the inner pocket of his heavy coat. Edith's eyes drifted toward the large clock on the wall. Almost time to go home.

It had been an incredibly busy day. Had it not been for the bank closing for lunch, she was sure that customers would have continued to pour through the door. With Christmas a few weeks away, they'd gotten much busier as people hurried in to withdraw funds before shopping.

Edith wished she could do the same. While she no longer had a family to purchase gifts for, she did have several close friends she'd made at the boarding house she'd lived in for the last two years. And then there was George. She'd always given him something at Christmas, and this year couldn't be any different.

Unfortunately, though she appreciated her job at the bank, there was very little left over after her rent and necessities. That was making the idea of surprising others at Christmas feel nearly impossible.

It wouldn't always be like that, Edith was sure. When the doctor's office she'd worked at for nearly five years had let her go unexpectedly due to their own financial situation, things had gotten difficult. Then, her mother grew ill, and every bit of the nest egg she'd saved went toward her mother's care.

She'd been so grateful to George for offering her this job. She'd withheld the troubles she had financially, even from him. Really, that wasn't too hard. Though she called George a friend—after all, they'd grown up together—he had a way of keeping to himself. He also wasn't the most observant of individuals. As a result, Edith wasn't sure he realized just how bad her situation was.

Yet, regardless of all her difficulties, Edith wouldn't change them for anything. The final months with her mother had been more than worth any suffering she might be experiencing now. It was only that it was nearly Christmas, a time filled with excitement and joy and bustling about that she was feeling a little melancholy about it.

She, too, wanted Christmas cheer and secrets and surprises to bestow upon others. Especially a beau or a husband. Neither of which was on the horizon. There had been a time she'd hoped George would ask for more than friendship, but he never had, and by now Edith had lost all hope. The fact no one else had even shown a shred of interest in her made Edith feel rather lonely at times.

"Finally," Mrs. Harpin, the head cashier, sighed and walked over to lock the bank's front door. "What a day!"

There were murmurs of agreement from the other four bank employees, Edith included. It had been. First, there was an unexpected dismissal of an employee—with the police there, no less! Afterward had been the never-ending stream of customers. Why, one had even pounded on the bank door ten minutes before opening.

Edith was grateful for the tall stools George had provided each of them at the counter. Otherwise, she knew her feet would be aching. Her shoes were getting a little worn out, and a small hole had developed in the bottom of one. Though she kept putting something inside to block the hole, it both rubbed at her foot and made the shoe fit strangely.

"Thank you, everyone," George said, walking into the bank lobby. He waited at the door to let them out, his bank key in his hand.

Edith collected her purse and came from behind the counter. Her shoes sounded loudly on the wooden boards of the floor as she crossed it.

The bank was quite spacious. In the lobby was a long counter with three windows that the tellers stood behind. Mrs. Harpin floated around wherever she was needed, as did Freddy, the assistant manager.

There were decorative metal bars over the windows protecting the money. While the bank had never been held up since she had been there, Edith wondered what measures could be done to protect them, if someone did come in with a pistol demanding the cash.

Luckily, the police station was next door, so perhaps that was a natural deterrent. At any rate, she'd never felt worried for her safety.

There were small rooms used as offices on the main floor of the bank, and a larger room that could be used as a meeting place with the wealthier customers. Safe deposit boxes were behind a thick door, and the vault was also hidden. Edith had never seen inside it herself.

A flight of stairs near the back led up to George's office, as well as a storage room. There was also a small break room upstairs for the employees. It was a good spot to heat a kettle of tea or enjoy one's lunch. George had thoughtfully provided a large table and chairs, as well as a storage area to keep their lunches until it was time.

Edith neared George and took a moment to study him. He was just a few months older than her. Quite handsome, he had dark blond hair that was wavy. Many women fluttered their eyelashes at him and flirted, but he didn't seem to notice. She dreaded the day he did, and perhaps even fell in love with one of them.

George was an incredibly hard worker, and the third-generation owner of the bank. He didn't ask for anything of his employees that he couldn't or wouldn't do himself. His father was just the same, and he oversaw several other banks. Eventually, George had told her, when his father retired, he'd be in charge of all eight.

The work sometimes wore on him, Edith could tell. She wished he would smile a little more often. Perhaps running a bank led to stresses and concerns or even an air of professionalism one must have, but Edith wasn't sure she'd seen many smiles from him, even though she'd been there nearly two years. His face was usually one of seriousness.

George used to smile more. His smiles had always lit up his eyes. She remembered how they'd laugh together over the smallest of things. Time had seemed to take that away, and Edith missed it. Slowly, as they'd grown up, George became more serious. Withdrawn. The rare smiles he flashed now melted something in her, the way they had when they were more frequent, back in their teenage years.

"Good afternoon, Edith," George told her as she walked past. "Thank you for your hard work today."

"I was happy to do it, and good afternoon," she answered, and stepped out into the sun-drenched town.

Richmond was a good-sized place. It was large enough to have many of the comforts and entertainments of larger cities, but was still small enough that you often passed a familiar face, and you needed not fear for your safety.

Edith lingered at shop windows as she walked toward her boarding house. There were new dresses in one, several children's toys, books, and games in another, and a selection of perfumes, soaps, and gloves in a third.

Greenery and Christmas ornaments mixed with ribbons and bows gave such a festive mood to her walk that Edith felt quite cheerful by the time she climbed the paint-chipped steps of the boarding house and pushed open the door.

The smell of dinner washed over her, and her stomach called out its excitement. Edith hurried to her room to set down her handbag to wash her hands.

The room was small, with a single bed and a chest of drawers across from it. A small table and hard chair rested in front of the medium-sized window, but it was affordable, clean, and the boarding house owner was a lovely woman who had become a friend.

The bell for dinner rang, the faint sound reaching her ears through the cracked door, and Edith hurried to join the others in the dining room. Over roasted chicken, boiled carrots, fried potatoes, and rolls, she listened to their chatter.

"What I really need," Mrs. Hedder, the boarding house owner, sighed, "is a Christmas miracle. If I could just get over there to see my boy, see for myself with my own two eyes how he is, it would set my mind at ease. After this accident, he and his wife have struggled so. And them with three small mouths to feed. I wish they'd come here. I've the room."

"Perhaps if you see them, they'll agree. It might be easier to persuade them in person," Widow Larson commented as she helped herself to another roll.

"I agree," Mrs. Hedder said, her brow pinched. "But I've not the funds."

"If I had them, I'd loan them to you," Widow Larson said. She sighed deeply. "I'd also get myself something I've been wanting."

"What's that?" Edith asked.

"A new shawl," she answered. "One with red roses on it." Widow Larson smiled dreamily. "Just the sort of thing to make me feel beautiful again."

"You are already beautiful," Edith said, "new shawl or not."

The older woman didn't answer, lost in her thoughts. Edith hoped she wasn't remembering the day she'd been attacked and the scars had been left on one side of her face. It had happened years before Edith had met her, but the other woman had since been shaken in her self-confidence.

"What of you?" Mrs. Hedder asked Mr. Rockingham, the third boarder. "What Christmas wish do you have?"

"Someone to keep me company," he said. "There is only so much reading one can do to fill the day. And what of you, Edith?"

She paused, her fork halfway to her lips, and lowered it. "I'm not sure," she finally answered. "I'll need to put more thought into it."

The chatter returned, and Edith frowned slightly. What she'd told the others wasn't quite true. She knew what she wanted. But she also knew she'd never be able to have it.

Chapter 2

George Alcott sat behind his desk, his elbows on the top, head resting in his hands. He was having a very bad day. The only bright spot was that the bank had closed ten minutes ago, and he was able to send everyone home, lock the door, and have a few moments to himself to indulge in self pity.

Even catching Edith Clarkson's eye as he'd said goodbye, and receiving a small smile from her, hadn't been enough. Usually, he looked forward to that. The smile he knew was just for him. But today...little was making him feel better. He was sure she had questions about what had happened earlier with the other employee and the police, but he hadn't been able to explain. The bank had been almost overwhelmingly busy.

It wasn't even a Monday. Those were usually the days when things went wrong. No, it was a Thursday. Perhaps the worst Thursday he could recall. First, the detective he had hired confirmed his worst suspicion. One of his employees was stealing from the bank.

The man had been escorted out by the police, but unfortunately, not only had his employees seen, and were unaware of the situation, which could, and likely would, lead to gossip among them, but it was possible that a few customers had too. There was little he could do about it, and the newspaper would surely have the details for anyone curious. But that was the least of his concerns.

That hadn't been the only difficult part of the day. After a severe storm last month, his home had taken damage to the roof. He'd hired someone—and paid half up front—for that repair and a few other small things to be done. After the man did not show up to complete the repairs, he discovered that his money had been taken and the man had disappeared. So, he was out of the money, still had a leaky roof, and it looked as though it would rain later today.

Just his luck.

George had experienced things like this repeatedly in his lifetime. One of his earliest childhood memories was of his parents warning him that if you have wealth, or even appear to have it, then someone is always out to take away part of it.

It was true. He didn't understand that. Where was the sense of pride in a job well done by a hard worker? Those individuals seemed too few and far between nowadays. A strong work ethic was something he'd been born with, inherited from his father and his grandfather before him. The Alcott men were a determined, focused group, and George was no exception.

But his experiences, whether they were personal or just observational, had led to him keeping to himself, trying to minimize him being taken advantage of. In all ways, he was cautious and, perhaps, even a little rigid.

It had kept him from forming meaningful relationships, and even his closest friend, Edith, he kept at a distance. He selfishly was glad when she'd lost her other job, and he'd been able to hire her at the bank. He hadn't needed her help, but he'd wanted her there.

George wanted Edith as more than just an employee or a friend. Far more. But he couldn't tell her that. Wouldn't even let himself think that. Besides the obvious—they were boss and employee—there was also the fact they were friends. There were too many reasons they hadn't ever become more, but on top of the rest of his worries today, George didn't dare let himself linger over them.

They'd lead to a deep pit of despair he would struggle to emerge from. As it was, he already spent too much time there.

He yawned, and then rubbed his hands together. There was a great deal to do. Just because the bank doors were closed didn't mean the day was done, especially for him.

George did not like to see people sitting around. He himself always kept busy. This time of year, though, it seemed a little harder to keep his employees focused. It was getting close to Christmas. Excited chatter hung in the air, but he did wish that they would keep their minds on the task at hand.

Thankfully, he had one employee who stood out above the rest and didn't indulge in time-wasting activities. Edith. She came to work on time, returned from lunch promptly, was personable and friendly with the customers, and took her job seriously. He appreciated that.

If he was also being perfectly honest with himself, he appreciated the fact that she was there. It made him happy to spend a moment here and there with her throughout the day. Though he still was strict with his emotions, there were times she'd bring an unexpected smile to his face, and he liked that. Appreciated it, even.

George raised his head, took a deep breath, and pushed back from the desk. Time to go home. Tomorrow would be different. Better.

He went down the bank lobby stairs, let himself out, and then checked that the door was locked. Strolling down the sidewalk, George let his eyes linger over all of the

Christmas items in the shop windows. As a child, he'd loved the season. As an adult...it was lonely.

Of course, he'd give a bonus to each of his employees. A gift was sent by post to his parents. But other than Edith, he had no friends or family nearby to shop for, to ponder over just the right gift for, then the pleasure of wrapping it, delivering it, and watching the recipient open it. He always loved exchanging gifts with Edith. It was difficult, though, as he couldn't get her the things he wanted to give her. They might be seen as too personal. Instead, he tried to find her gifts that would bring her pleasure, and hoped he succeeded.

The reminder of the quiet, empty house he'd be going to made him feel even lonelier. It was his own fault, some would say. He had offers of romance, but he didn't want them. Who he wanted, he couldn't have.

George turned his head up to the sky. It had grown much colder these last few weeks. Likely, there would be snow soon. A chilling wind blew, and he turned up his collar and hurried toward his house.

He lived not far from the bank, in a small house that had been snug until his roof problems. George let himself in, and followed his nose to the kitchen. A pot of stew simmered over the wood oven.

Mrs. Muddles, his daytime housekeeper, had left a note. He scanned it, and then set it down. She'd wished him a pleasant meal, and let him know there was a cake freshly made under a clean cloth for his enjoyment as well.

George ate his dinner while reading the newspaper. He'd already read it that day during lunch, but reading it again gave him something to do and focus on other than his solitude.

No surprise, the paper was filled with tidbits about the upcoming holidays. Merchants had taken out ads, talking about their selection of goods. He browsed them, wondering what he should get Edith.

With a sigh, George set down the paper, put his dish and spoon into the sink for Mrs. Muddles to wash tomorrow, and retired to his study.

The rest of the evening was spent going over files from the bank, double checking the ledger, and making himself a note to seek someone trustworthy to fix his roof.

Recently, he'd become friendly with the general store owner, Jake Smith. He was a practical man. Perhaps he could recommend an honest repairman. He'd had some work done on his own building recently, hadn't he?

George absently watched through the window as people hurried past in groups of two or three. Almost all of them were smiling. What would that be like? Having someone to talk and laugh with? He used to, back when he was younger, and he and Edith had spent more time together. He'd always thought they'd be together, perhaps even marry. But as the years passed, somewhere along the way, he'd missed his chance. Eventually, his words froze entirely, and they just settled into friendship.

"Doesn't matter. That's not for me," George said firmly, closing his curtain.

No, he'd never find romance. There were too many people out there wanting to take advantage of a person to get too close. Today had been a double lesson in that. Who knew what tomorrow would bring? Likely more of the same.

Chapter 3

Edith smoothed her skirt, then ran her hands down it again. She was on her lunch hour, and knew George was in his office. Her heart was pounding at the idea of what she was about to do, but Edith took a deep breath, raised her hand, and knocked timidly on the door.

She had no idea why she was scared. They'd known each other for years. George wouldn't bite her head off, so why was she worried? Her attempt at reassuring herself didn't work, and butterflies took flight in her stomach. It was good she hadn't eaten yet.

"Come in."

Though only two words, they made her hands tremble. All last night, Edith had rehearsed what she wanted to say. How she was going to ask. But now that the moment was here, she had completely forgotten every word.

Edith pushed open the door, willing herself to look and act calm. There was no reason for him to know that she was as nervous as she was.

"Edith," he said, looking at her in surprise. She watched as he pushed aside the ledger he'd been hovering over, and set down his pen. "Er, I-I wasn't expecting you. What can I do for you? Is something wrong downstairs?" George ran his hand over his hair.

"No," she answered quickly, hoping she hadn't distracted him from something important by the way he was stammering. "I'm on my lunch. I came here on a personal matter. Well, business as well. Personal business." Edith tried not to cringe at her own stammering. She hated how she did that when she was nervous, and right now she was very nervous.

"Oh?" He raised his brows and motioned to one of the cushioned chairs before his desk. "Have a seat. This sounds important."

Edith sat, then tried not to run her hands down her skirts again. Her stomach was fluttering twice as much, but she pushed the feeling down, praying the butterflies within her would settle before her nausea got any worse.

"What can I do for you?" George asked.

Edith tried not to shiver as his warm eyes turned to her. This wasn't the first time she'd ever been alone with him entirely. A familiar thought fluttered through her mind. She'd often wondered what it would be like to be alone with him every day, in a house of their own. The moment she thought that, she frowned and refocused, turning her thoughts to the matter at hand.

"I wanted to know if I could take out a loan," Edith answered. Her words were rushed from nerves, but she managed to speak them.

"A loan. From the bank?" His head tipped to the side slightly as he waited for her response.

"Yes."

He was quiet for a moment. "Well, perhaps. Typically, when a loan is written, there is some sort of collateral put up. That is the rule. And...then—though I don't agree—there is the fact you are a woman and a loan would be...most unusual. I'd like to help if I can, though. What would you be offering as collateral?"

"Collateral?" Edith asked in a small voice.

"Yes. Something of some value that assures the bank that you will return the funds loaned, or else surrender the item in exchange." He folded his hands and rested them on his desk. "For example, property. Jewelry."

"Oh." She sat very still for a moment, then gave a small shrug. "I...I don't have anything of value, otherwise I'd have sold it. That's why I needed a loan," Edith explained. Quickly, she added, "But I don't need a large one. And I am sure I can pay it back from my salary within a few months."

"That's not how loans work," he told her. "There is a minimum amount for the loan, and also the collateral." George studied her for a moment, and Edith tried not to squirm. "What is it you wish the loan for? Perhaps there is another way the bank can help. After all, you are a valued employee. If I can assist, I will."

"I'd like to get Christmas gifts," Edith answered.

"Christmas gifts." George stared at her flatly. "And that isn't something you can do on your pay? You need to take out a loan?"

"Well, these gifts are...one is rather large..." Edith knew she was stammering.

He shook his head. "I'm sorry. Without collateral, the bank won't be able to help." His lips twitched, as though he were holding back a smile. "You'll simply have to scale back your holiday shopping. Perhaps skip giving gifts this year or buy more inexpensive items."

Her face flamed. Edith stood quickly. Mortification filled her, and she squeezed her hands together. It was obvious, by the expression on his face and the tone of his words, he thought her nothing more than a silly girl who was frivolous with her money.

She wanted to argue, wanted to explain, but was sure anything she said now would be ignored. That is, if she could even say anything past the tears wanting to form. She'd never been so embarrassed in her life. She'd been foolish to think her friend would help. All she wanted to do now was escape.

"I'm sorry to have wasted your time," Edith said, her voice tight.

"Edith, wait. You know I want to help if I can. Perhaps the bank can't, but I can." George reached a hand out, then dropped it.

"No, never mind." Before he could say another word, and before she humiliated herself further, Edith hurried from the office and shut the door behind her.

The rest of the afternoon passed agonizingly slowly. Edith's mind replayed the incident with George over and over. The unfairness of it all bothered her. She supposed she could have protested more. Explained why she wanted the loan. How she intended to pay it back.

But when he'd insinuated that her problem was that she spent too much...And then, of course, there was the fact she couldn't remember all she'd wanted to say. How she wanted to convince him.

Edith fought back tears. She didn't spend too much. No penny was wasted. That's why her feet ached from her worn shoes, and her dresses, though always clean, were faded and starting to become threadbare in spots. George should know what kind of a person she was!

But he was right. The more she thought about it, the more she knew she'd been foolish, thinking that she could ask for a loan with nothing to show to assure she'd pay it back. Truth be told, though she had every intention, it would be difficult to repay the loan. A sacrifice would have to be made, but what more could she do?

It's just she wanted, more than anything, to make Christmas special for her friends. She knew what it was like to be lonely and worried and...and if she could bring them happiness, then perhaps she'd feel her own sorrow less. There was also the matter of George's gift. She wanted to find something to bring a smile to his face. That would cost more than she had.

Edith knew she didn't need to spend anything to make her friends feel valued, but she wanted to. She wanted to give a gift that would bring joy, give comfort. She wanted, more than anything, to make others happy so that they could have a wonderful Christmas season.

The lump in her throat ached, and it stayed with her the rest of the afternoon. When the workday was over, she hurried out the door, her head low, and not answering George's goodbye. It would be better to let today be over with. To forget that it happened.

She also didn't want to remember the look on his face. He'd smirked at her.

Until today, she'd enjoyed when he'd told her goodbye, as he said it to her differently from the others. It had made her wonder if perhaps he'd finally grown some small affection for her. That maybe that was why he'd linger near her at times, ask her to do a small task, instead of someone else.

All of those thoughts fled the moment she'd seen his face. Now, she never wanted to go back. But that was also ridiculous. She had to. There were expenses to pay.

What a fool she was. Asking for a loan, secretly harboring feelings for her boss and friend. He'd never think of her in that way. No one did.

She was nothing and no one. Just a poor, penniless bank employee, with a hole in her shoe and a matching one in her heart.

Chapter 4

He'd handled that badly. George groaned as the office door shut, and the sound of Edith's footsteps rushed away. He'd meant his words to come out as a jest. Edith was one of the most careful and conscientious individuals he knew. Of course she wouldn't be frivolous with her shopping.

Likely, she'd only wanted a few dollars. But he'd stupidly not even asked her how much she needed. Blast his tongue! It betrayed him at the worst times. George knew he couldn't be more upset at himself than he was right now.

It was true what he'd said about collateral. It was a bank rule. But there surely would have been a way. Why was he such a fool? He never had difficulty talking to others, not even women.

Except for her. Something about Edith usually made his tongue feel like it was flopping about ridiculously, and he was jabbering and not making the least bit of sense. Just like when she'd come into his office earlier. Why, if it weren't for the fact he told her good afternoon each day, and his brain had gotten quite used to it, he'd likely mess that up as well!

He walked to the window and surveyed the town below. People hurried past, eager to get out of the cold or into the stores for their shopping.

Shopping. Now he'd regret not loaning her even a little. What if she'd just been saying she wanted it for Christmas shopping? Using the holiday as an excuse? What if she had dire need of money for something else, but had been too embarrassed to say so? He knew she needed a warmer shawl, new shoes, warmer dresses. While she'd never mentioned that, he observed those things about her.

George observed everything about Edith, and had from the day he'd met her. Especially as of late. The smile that sometimes didn't meet her eyes. Her endless kindness to even the most trying of customers. The dark circles under her eyes that spoke of perhaps an evening job to make more money or worries that he knew nothing about.

And here she'd actually come to him, her friend, asking for help and he'd bungled the entire thing. What was wrong with him?

With a frustrated sigh, George threw open his office door and strode into the employee break room to seek her. He'd fix this, somehow.

But when he stuck his head in, an excuse for her at the ready, Edith wasn't there. Her lunch break must have been over. He started down the stairs. If she'd allow him, perhaps he could make it a personal loan. He couldn't break the bank rules, but a loan between friends?

Who was he kidding? George's shoulders slumped. She likely would never want to talk to him again. He'd embarrassed her. He hadn't meant to, but he had, just the same. Though she'd turned almost instantly, he hadn't missed her stricken expression, nor the sob that had wrenched free.

His step faltered as he neared the bottom of the stairs. No, he couldn't offer her anything at all, even as a friend. If he were to do that, then everyone who worked there—even those who were not as responsible as Edith—would expect him to do something like that for them. And if he did, or even if he didn't, simply offering that to her might put them in a position of gossip.

The last thing that George wanted to do was to compromise Edith's reputation. He'd already wounded her pride. He didn't need to do anything else to her. A woman's reputation was more easily damaged than a man's was. He'd always thought that unfair, but that was the way it was.

If he'd thought yesterday was bad, today was much worse. And this time, it was all because of his actions, not those of another.

He stopped on the last stair. Edith was helping an older couple. Her face was sweet, her voice calm and polite. He watched her for a short time, then turned and headed back up the stairs before she saw him. What could he say to her?

Nothing.

As he neared the employee break room, he heard something that made him freeze.

"He told her no! An absolute Scrooge," he recognized one of the male employees saying. "Don't know why he refused. This is a bank, isn't it? Edith is a hard-working employee."

"Sal was too," a woman answered, "and see how he was dragged out yesterday by the police?"

"I heard he was taking money from the bank," another voice said in a loud whisper. "Maybe it's good he's gone."

"Doesn't excuse making Edith cry," the woman said firmly.

George hurried back to his office and shut the door. His stomach felt sick, and he let out a shuddering breath. He'd made her cry. He hadn't meant to! What a mess he'd gotten himself into.

Hurting Edith was the last thing he wanted. Spending more time with her...that was what he'd longed for, dreamed of. In fact, that's what he had wanted long before she'd ever started working for him. From the moment he'd first run into her at the general store so many years ago, knocking her purchases out of her hands as he was backing up to get a better look at something on a low shelf, he knew there was something about her he found irresistible. They'd become friends instantly.

His heart had started to thump loudly the moment she walked in seeking work. He readily agreed to hire her, and how he'd hoped there would be a chance to pick up again where they'd never quite made it to. But each and every time, without fail, he stopped himself from becoming too close.

Stopped himself because he was tired of being taken advantage of. Because he was scared it would happen again. Scared that if there was a betrayal from the woman he'd thought about constantly, he couldn't bear it.

"But this feeling is worse," George muttered, opening a desk drawer and rummaging through it.

The best thing to do would be to forget about today. Forget about Edith, their conversation, the way he felt toward her, how stupid he'd been.

But he couldn't forget about her. They'd known each other too long. She was someone he could easily see himself with. It was too late for that now. If only he'd never hired her. Then he wouldn't have made such a mistake. He'd have helped her, made sure her Christmas was merry. But if he hadn't hired her...she might have also moved on. Not been here, where he could see her almost every day. The whole thing was his fault. He should have asked her years before to court. Now, he'd wasted his chance. And after today, Edith might never speak to him unless it was pertaining to her job.

George shook his head slowly. How was he ever going to be able to close his eyes again, without seeing the hurt on her face that he caused? The very thought was devastating.

Chapter 5

"He told you no?" Mrs. Hedder shook her head as she set more dishes next to the soapy water. "And after you've worked there so hard and not asked for a thing! Why, the two of you are good friends, I thought. He isn't even willing to help his friend?"

Edith sighed as she plunged her hands into the warm, soapy water, wetting a bowl. "As I think more about it, really there was no way that he could have said yes."

"Humph. A kinder soul than I'd be, that's what you are," Mrs. Hedder answered. "The very nerve of that man. I declare, what was he thinking? I'd like to go down and give him a piece of my mind."

"It's quite all right," Edith said with a half smile. "As soon as I asked, I knew it was a bad idea. Though it was embarrassing, both asking and hearing his answer. I don't know how I'll be able to look him in the face again. What must he think of me?"

"I heard the hotel is hiring," Mrs. Hedder said. "I don't know what positions, but I bet it's are a good place to work."

"I like my job, though," Edith said in a deep sigh. "If possible, I'd like to stay there. I'll just figure out something else for the extra that I need right now. And, I plan to try and avoid George, if possible. At least until some of the sting leaves his words."

"What is it you are wanting to buy?" Mrs. Hedder asked curiously.

Edith just shrugged. She wasn't about to tell Mrs. Hedder she was trying to make the woman's Christmas wish come true!

"This and that," she said, then added, "I did pick up a little sewing in the evening. The dressmaker wanted someone to help her with piecework."

"Just don't work yourself to death," Mrs. Hedder said. She dried the last dish and shook her head as she put them into the cabinet. "Being an adult is hard. Used to be when we were children, we'd write to Santa, and wait for all our wishes to come true."

Edith laughed. "Indeed! I remember a few of those letters," she said as she recalled them. There had been the year she'd asked for a pony. One year, it was a doll she could dress up. Another, some books.

"Never too old to enjoy Christmas, and all the magic it brings," Mrs. Hedder said, wiping her hands on her apron. "Even if you don't get a reply, there's the fun of writing the letter and letting yourself dream a little bit." She untied the apron and hung it on a hook near the stove.

"You are right," Edith agreed.

Mrs. Hedder left, and as Edith stood there alone in the kitchen, a strange idea came to mind. Why not write Santa again? Oh, of course nothing would come of it. Santa wasn't for grownups...but perhaps just the act of writing the letter, combined with all of her hard work, she could make her friends' Christmas wishes come true. Mrs. Hedder was correct. There was both the fun of writing it and the dreaming that could come about.

She'd write it, but only after she started on that project for the dressmaker. Since Santa couldn't answer her letter, she still had to rely upon herself to make their wishes come true.

Two hours later, in her room and ready for bed, Edith sat with a candle flickering, dropping shadows on her sheet of paper. She thought for a long moment, then started to write.

Dear Santa,

I don't know if you remember me. As a child, I had the most wonderful of Christmases, in part because of you, my parents said. I could use your help again this year. Not for myself, but for three of the kindest people I know.

I admit, I feel a little silly writing to you. What would others think if they knew? But I am feeling desperate. It is my hope that writing this letter eases the sting of the day, and helps me clear my mind to solve my problem.

You see, today, I asked for a loan from the bank I work for. The answer was no. I won't go into how humiliated I felt, but no matter the answer, I'm determined to bring Christmas cheer to my friends.

They have been through so much over the last few years, and I want to make Christmas special for them. I took a job sewing at night from the dressmaker, as caring for my mother in her final illness took all I had saved. I just need a little extra Christmas magic this year to make everything work out.

First is the boarding house owner, Mrs. Hedder. She's desperate to see her son this Christmas. After an accident, he isn't healing well, and can't travel. He's several hours away, right outside Midway here in Kentucky, but she's anxious to see him for herself, and hopes she can help him, his wife, and their three young children, perhaps by even bringing them here.

Next is Widow Larson. She wants a shawl with red roses on it. I saw one at the general store that I want to save up to buy her. It was in the shop window, but the price, though reasonable, is more than I have. She says she'd feel so beautiful wearing it. She deserves that. A few years ago, she escaped someone who attacked her, but ended up with scars on her face. She's still beautiful, but refuses to believe it.

Lastly, there is dear Mr. Rockingham. I couldn't tell you how old he is, and neither would he. He's terribly lonely. About a year ago, he moved to the boarding house after his wife of many decades passed away. They never had children, so he has very little companionship. Though he lives at the boarding house, he does have many hours in the day where he needs someone to keep him company.

That is my list, dear Santa, foolish as it might seem.

Please, help me in some way to bring my friends the happiness they deserve, even if it's simply that you help me find the strength and determination to do what I need to do to bring it about. They are good people, and this is the time of year when joyfulness tends to mix with sadness. For them, I'd rather the former.

Faithfully,

Edith Clarkson

Edith read over her letter, then shook her head at her foolishness. Writing a letter to Santa—and at her age!

But, she thought as she folded it and set it near her shoes to post to the North Pole tomorrow, it was the time of year when goodness abounded, and miracles happened. Perhaps one more would. Edith gave a small laugh. It must, for she didn't have a mailing address for Santa, and would simply have to have faith it would get to where it needed to go.

She blew out the candle, climbed into bed, and her eyes sought the night sky through the second-floor window. Stars twinkled, and she admired the moon's dim light. Edith closed her eyes, trying to feel the peaceful tiredness that usually filled her.

However, tonight, she kept shifting to get comfortable, and block the memories of earlier that day. Never had she been so embarrassed. She'd known George for a long time, and, yes, sometimes he blurted out things without thinking, but today was just terrible. It was almost as if he didn't know her at all.

Edith wistfully imagined what it would have been like if, years before, she'd been brave enough to ask him for more than friendship. She'd thought he was interested in her. He'd seemed that way. Had she really been wrong? A time or two he'd gazed at her with such a look it nearly burned through her. Once, he'd even reached for her hand. Then he'd stopped. Why?

The hours she'd thought about him. More than hours. Months. Years. But it was obvious he hadn't thought about her. Except for that she had a spending problem!

Edith's eyes narrowed. She'd show him! She didn't need the bank to give her a loan. There was extra work to be done and—her eyes sought the direction of the letter—Santa was on her side. A real man or not, the thought of her letter bolstered her in some way.

Call her foolish; she didn't care. This would be the best Christmas ever for her friends, Edith was sure of it. Perhaps she'd even find some measure of happiness for herself.

Chapter 6

"You know what your problem is?" Jake Smith asked as he set down his mug.

"No, but I've the feeling you're about to tell me," George laughed.

He didn't mind, though. Jake Smith, the general store owner, was as honest as they came. He was also a man with an additional job very few knew about. Jake was an FBI agent. It was on his recommendation that George hired the detective to help stop the employee who had been stealing from the bank. The detective was a former FBI agent, and a good friend of Jake's.

As interesting as Jake was, his wife Louise might have been even more fascinating. A few months before, she'd helped stop an international gang of thieves and blackmailers—in fact, she'd been engaged to the leader at one point. That was before she'd discovered the truth and escaped on the *Titanic*. She hadn't reckoned the man would follow her, but he had.

Her sister's story was also quite interesting. Who'd have thought their small town would have had such excitement?

"The problem is," Jake said, "sometimes a position leads to a natural distance. It must. It's not that no one likes you. But if you really want people to know who you are, you can't always hide yourself."

"Easy for you to say," George grumbled, then took a bite of his sandwich. "Everyone likes you. And you know everyone."

"Because I'm approachable." Jake shrugged. "I work in a store. It's also my job to be amicable. Besides, people like you."

"Yes, but they aren't friendly. And yes, I know that's my fault," George sighed. "It's become second nature to keep that wall around myself."

Jake nodded. "I understand what it's like to have to put a distance between yourself and those who work for you or those you are trying to protect. I also understand what it's like to be taken advantage of because of the position you hold."

"It's not a good feeling," George said. "You feel as though you are often on the outside looking in. But, it's due to necessity."

"Sometimes it is," Jake agreed. "Worse when you have money or work around money, I expect. Sometimes others think because you have something, even if you're not well off, that they should have it too. It doesn't make it right for them to think that, but it also is something you may have to accept and find a way around in order to have meaningful relationships and build friendships."

"That's easier said than done," George answered heavily.

"I know, but if you don't, you're going to be very lonely." Jake studied him for a moment. "Do you want to settle down one day? With a family?"

"I'd like to," George admitted. "There's even someone I like. Just..." He shook his head.

"You're scared to tell her?" Jake prodded.

"That, because I don't know what her reaction would be, but also because around her, my brain and my tongue don't quite connect. My mouth starts spitting out things I didn't intend."

Jake laughed and slapped the table. A few people looked over at them curiously. "Never thought you'd do that," he said.

"Yes, well, I'm full of surprises," George answered wryly.

Jake shrugged. "If it's meant to be, a way will come about to bring you together. I'm sure of that. As for the other stuff...

no need to rush into anything. Just think about it. That's all."

George nodded, and was glad that Jake sensed his unwillingness to talk further. The rest of their lunch was spent on lighter conversation, but as George headed back to the bank, he realized that all Jake had said was true.

Not only that, he was already lonely, though he hadn't admitted that to Jake. There was a hollow feeling deep inside, and it hadn't ever been filled. He wasn't even sure it could be. Had he kept himself separated for so long that there was no chance of finding someone to make him feel complete and content?

The person he'd wanted, he'd now hurt. He'd never forgive himself for that. Or for the fact he might have lost any chance of being with her in the future. It was bad enough he'd hesitated so often that she was no longer interested in him, but now, as well as he knew Edith, he imagined she wouldn't even meet his eye the next time they saw each other. Life was bleak, and this time of year, when cheerfulness filled the streets, it felt even worse.

Sure, he'd been invited to holiday events. But he didn't miss the fact that often when there was a social event, others didn't come up and include him in conversation, unless it was about business or there was a charity fund they needed a donation for. And perhaps that was a side effect of him always keeping himself business-focused and separate from others. It also could simply be as he'd always suspected. It was his connections or money that people wanted. That's why he tended to linger in the shadows. Watch others enjoy themselves.

But how could he change that? Did he want to? A small part of him did, but he wasn't sure where to start.

George opened the bank's door, and nodded at his employees as he made his way over to the stairs. Edith didn't look his way, and his stomach sank. It was just as he thought. She likely still felt embarrassed. He needed to fix that too. He didn't want to lose her in his life. But again, the question was how.

He went to his office and glanced through the stack of mail waiting. Then an idea formed. He took up his pen, replying to the letters and notices that had been sent to him as quickly as he reasonably could.

George's heart sped up as a hint of excitement formed. He'd call Edith up here under the pretense of taking the mail to the post, as she sometimes did, and use the opportunity to make amends. It sounded so simple, even if he wasn't sure she'd look at him, and simple plans were the ones that worked best. Usually. That meant he stood a chance, no matter how small it was.

He finished, and then stuck his head into the hallway. Luckily, Freddy, the head teller, was passing by. "Would you please ask Edith to come to my office?" he asked.

The man nodded and hurried down the stairs while George returned to his desk to wait. His fingers were nervous as he straightened and then straightened again the stack of mail. A lump formed in his throat, and just as quickly dropped to his stomach when there was a knock on his door.

Chapter 7

The air that morning on her way to work had been biting, and soft snow flurries had speckled everything they touched. Edith had brushed herself off before walking into the bank building. Once there, she sagged in relief at the welcoming warmth.

That was another reason she'd always enjoyed working here. George didn't spare any expense in keeping the building warm. He did it both for the employees and the customers, even though he knew his employees would benefit the most.

Edith rubbed her hands together. They were stiff from the cold. Her gloves were quite thin. Though she longed for a new pair, spring would arrive in a few months. She could make do. Perhaps next year.

"Chilly, isn't it?" Susan Cooper asked as she took her spot behind the counter.

"Yes. If the wind weren't blowing, I think it wouldn't be so bad," Edith answered as she removed her scarf and shawl. "I'll be right back. Just going to hang these up."

Edith walked up the stairs, set her belongings down, and returned to take her place behind the counter.

"You coming to the Christmas party?" Susan asked Edith.

The bank Christmas party was a large affair. George paid for food to be brought in, and for a trio of violinists to play music. The employees were each allowed to invite one other if they wanted, and it was always a fun and festive event.

"I am," Edith answered. "Is your husband able to attend this year?"

"Charlie's thrown out his back again. I hope he'll be able to. I don't plan to miss out. A shame, though," Susan said, and stopped to help a customer.

Once the customer had left, Edith asked, "A shame, what? About Charlie?"

"No. A shame George will be there. He always just stands around watching everyone."

"That's not very nice," Edith said, then startled at her defense. But it was true. It wasn't. Even if he just stood and watched. "He always gives a lovely party, and a Christmas bonus."

A Christmas bonus! She'd forgotten about that! It wouldn't be enough to get Mrs. Hedder to her son, but it would still be enough to get each of her friends something special. Though it wouldn't be what they most longed for, she could at least give something to brighten their day. Her heart sped up in excitement. Susan's grunt of disagreement brought her back to the present.

"Besides," Edith continued, "he deserves to be there. He pays for it all and is the owner. I wonder..." She frowned then, her brow furrowing so hard her forehead ached. "I wonder if perhaps he's unsure how to talk to people. If he feels awkward because he's the boss."

"You find the good in everyone," Susan sniffed. "When will you see some people have none?"

"Surely you don't mean that! And especially not about George," Edith said firmly.

"I guess I don't," Susan agreed reluctantly. "He has always been a kind and reasonable employer."

"I—"

"Edith, the boss wants you," Freddy said as he hurried past with an armful of ledgers.

"Oh, I'd better go see what it is," Edith said, sounding far more cheerful than she felt.

Why did he want to see her? Was he going to humiliate her again?

Her legs felt heavy as she forced them up the stairs. Every bit of her seemed to resist walking closer. Finally, she stood outside of his office door and, after slowly counting to twenty, knocked.

"Come in," George called.

Edith opened the door and stepped inside, leaving the door ajar. She tried to look at anything but him. "You wanted to see me?"

"Yes, I did." His chair scraped, and as she looked over to see him stand, their eyes caught.

"Edith," he started, then stopped. He was swallowing hard, and his face was filled with worry. It cleared then, that perfectly smooth mask he was so good at wearing slipping over his face. "I asked for you," he continued, "for two reasons. The first is I'd like you to take this stack of mail to the post office for me."

"Of course," she said, reaching to take it when he offered it to her. She could mail her letter at the same time.

Their fingers brushed, and Edith's breath caught at the tingle through her fingers. Her eyes lowered, and she waited, terrified that the quivering in her stomach might make its way to her voice. Though years had passed, that fluttering in her stomach from an accidental brush renewed itself.

There was a long moment, and nothing was said. The air felt heavy. Almost suffocating. They each stood, nearly frozen, their hands on the mail.

It seemed he felt it as well, for George cleared his throat. "About that loan. I want to apologize," he said.

"There's no need," Edith answered him firmly as she pulled the mail from his grasp.

"No, there is. I think what I intended as a jest came out wrong. In fact," he ran a hand through his thick hair, "So much of what I often say comes out wrong. I'm sorry."

His face was so earnest, his eyes so serious, that Edith instantly softened. She understood. After all, who hadn't said something they regretted, meaning it as a joke? It eased her embarrassment slightly.

"There's nothing to apologize for," she insisted, "though I appreciate it. You were quite right, in that I don't have collateral for a loan."

"It's not that," he said, and paced to the window before he turned back. "I mean about the shopping jest, especially. I don't know why I said that. I..."

His face looked so stricken, Edith knew she couldn't hold anything against him. Every ounce of the humiliation she'd felt the previous day vanished, replaced with an emotion she didn't quite understand. Compassion mixed with concern.

She stepped closer and joined him at the window. "George, I was embarrassed, yes, but I understand now you didn't mean for it to come out the way it did. I know we are also friends, and that I need to be careful not to take advantage of that."

"That's just it. We *are* friends," he said. "First and foremost. I'd still like to help," he told her. "The bank can't give you a loan, but I—"

"No," Edith said firmly. "People would talk."

It was true. And not something she wanted. The others who worked there would ask why he was paying her special favor. Even if they kept it secret, the truth would come out, and that would be even more damaging, to both of them.

"I don't know the circumstances," George said slowly, "though I recognize that determination in you. Is there some way I can help you?"

"I am going to figure it out." Edith shrugged. "Somehow. You'll laugh, I know, but I've written a letter to Santa. I am also working at night for a seamstress."

His eyes widened, but George didn't say anything. He still looked doubtful, but his expression wasn't one of pity or disparaging. "Santa. I see. You would ask me, though, if I could help in some way? I'd...I'd like the chance to make things up to you."

"You don't need to," Edith said. "It's Christmastime, and I believe that something good will happen this year to those I care about. I need it too."

Edith closed her eyes against the tears that wanted to fall. When she opened them, George was looking at her with such concern, an unwanted tear fell.

"What's wrong?" he asked quietly.

With a deep breath, Edith explained, "This will be a very difficult Christmas because it will be the first one that I have been truly all alone. This was my mother's favorite time of year, and since she passed away, it's not quite felt the same. So, by focusing on others and how I can help them, I'm hoping it will help me as well."

"By helping them," his voice was just above a whisper, his gaze distant, "you help yourself..." He didn't seem to realize he'd spoken, but met her eyes. "I'm sorry for the loss of your mother, and the pain the season brings to those who are without friendship, family, or that which they need. I should have been more understanding. I'm sorry. I've been so busy working, I've not been a proper friend, thinking about your pain."

"Pain is part of life," Edith told him. "It's part of what helps us enjoy the good times."

"You have given me so much to think on," George said. His gaze drifted to the window. He snapped his attention back to her a moment later. "You have always forgiven me so quickly during our friendship. May I ask why?"

Edith was quiet for a moment, then said, "Years ago, something my grandmother said left a lasting impression upon me. Before she passed away, she spoke of her one regret, and that was her pride stopping her from accepting the apology of someone. It grew too late to make amends, as she'd lost contact with the person. But I vowed to never do the same." Edith swallowed hard. "No matter how difficult that might be. Besides, is it not the season for goodwill toward men?"

George nodded slowly. "Your grandmother was very wise. You as well. Thank you, Edith. I am grateful for your kindness and for the good number of years we have known each other."

She wasn't sure how to answer, and simply smiled. "I'll get these sent for you now. I had my letter to post, so I was going there anyway."

Edith left, her heart feeling much lighter. All she'd said was true, and she could tell that he hadn't meant to hurt or embarrass her. There was a sense of relief too, in that now she didn't need to consider getting work elsewhere.

Perhaps things would work out. She was feeling better about the entire situation. Though she and George had rarely had misunderstandings, they'd always been able to put differences behind them. This would be no different.

Freddy came up the stairs just as she was about to go down and bumped into her.

"Sorry, Edith," he apologized, trying to look around the stack of boxes he was carrying. "Did you drop something?"

"Just the mail to go out," Edith said. "I've got it, never you mind. It was an accident."

She stooped and quickly collected the letters, then stopped at Susan's counter. "I need to take these to the post office. I'll be back shortly."

The other woman nodded, and Edith started across the lobby. The door opened just as she got there.

"Sam!" she greeted the mail carrier. "I was about to take these to the post office."

"I've got them, Miss Edith," he said, taking the letters from her hand. He handed her a small package addressed to the bank and tipped his hat. "Good day."

Edith watched him go, some of the weight from her shoulders gone. Her letter to Santa was on its way, she was feeling better about her previous interaction with George, and everything was feeling much better.

Christmas magic must already be at work.

Chapter 8

George locked the door behind the last employee, and nodded to the night guard. "I'll be leaving shortly," he said.

"Let me know when," the guard requested.

"I will," George answered, and headed toward the stairs to get his coat. Today, he wasn't in a hurry to stay behind in the office.

Though he was feeling better that Edith wasn't upset at him any longer, he was tired, as he'd hardly slept the night before for worry over their conversation.

His lips quirked into a smile as he recalled their earlier conversation. Though it had been brief, her confiding that she was mailing a letter to Santa couldn't help but make him chuckle. He had kept his face neutral, but it made him like her all the more, that she hadn't lost the childlike wonder of the holiday season. What would it be like to be around someone like that every day? He could just imagine it. Coming home, and seeing that Edith had the house decorated beautifully for Christmas. Together, they'd decorate a tree and—

What was he doing? He had no right at all to think such a thing about her. She was his friend and employee. Nothing more. Could never be anything more. He'd seen to that. First, he'd wasted his chances with her years ago, then he'd humiliated her when she'd sought his help. Yes, she'd forgiven him, but that didn't change much. They were back where they started, boss and employee and childhood friends, and no chance of anything more.

He wished there could be, though. Then George could comfort her in her sorrow over the loss of her mother. He could make sure she wasn't alone, or sad, or in need of something, both now and always. He should have done that already. Should have thought about how she was suffering. He'd been too wrapped up in his work, though.

There was an ache in his heart at the thought, and George rubbed at his chest. Would he always hurt when he thought about Edith? Probably. There wasn't anyone else who had caught his attention. He couldn't imagine anyone ever holding a higher position in his mind or heart.

Releasing a yawn, he climbed the steps, then paused as he spotted a glimpse of white at the base of the railing. It was a letter. One must have fallen as someone had carried them.

As he picked up the envelope, he noted the back wasn't closed. He flipped it over to see who was intended to receive the letter, and his eyes widened. There, in the beautiful penmanship he recognized as Edith's, was written:

Santa Claus, North Pole

"Oh no! Her letter didn't get mailed," George said. He frowned. The boarding house was nearby. Should he return it there? He could also simply mail it for her. Yes, that would be the better choice. She might not want others to see the letter.

He returned to his desk to get his coat, fully intending to take it to the post office, but as he glanced at the envelope once more, intense curiosity filled him, and he peeked at the letter. It was folded, of course, but...perhaps just a small, quick glimpse? She might not mind. In fact, if he'd asked, perhaps earlier she'd have shown him.

George was more than curious as to what it was that Edith had wanted for Christmas. He pulled the letter free, and a tiny flash of guilt filled him as he did. It was wrong to read someone else's mail, even if it wasn't sealed, or was sitting out. He knew that. He also knew, if he thought about it too hard, that Edith wouldn't have shared what was in the letter. She didn't in person.

He ought to put the letter back, seal the envelope, and mail it.

But he unfolded the sheet of paper anyway. As he skimmed it and came to the end, George found himself sitting in his chair, and reading it again slowly, from the top.

Swallowing hard, he set the letter on his desk. Edith's letter had been so full of desire to help others. She hadn't thought of herself at all. George took a moment to calculate. While she'd mentioned to Santa she was taking in extra work, that, even with the Christmas bonus he would give, wouldn't be enough to help her fulfill those Christmas wishes.

She really did need a Christmas miracle. Or Santa to help her.

George folded the letter, feeling discouraged as he put it back into the envelope. Had she also felt sad as she'd written the letter? He rose. There was still time to post it for her. It was a shame that there would be no answer to her letter.

He shrugged on his coat and had crossed to his office door when he froze. "Why not?" he whispered as the idea started to form. "Why can't Santa help?"

Turning, he hurried back to his desk, pulled out a sheet of paper, and took up his pen. Careful to disguise his handwriting, he wrote three short lines.

Ms. Clarkson, your letter has been received. Let me see what I can do. But you neglected to mention...what do you want for Christmas?

Santa

His heart was thumping as he folded the note, wrote her address on it, and placed it in the chest pocket of his overcoat. What would she think when she got the reply?

George walked out into the evening air. It had grown quite cold, and everyone who was still out hurried, collars turned against the damp chill. He couldn't help but stare at each, wondering about their stories. Both his and Edith's conversation today, and reading Edith's letter, had showed him something he should have known, had known, but had, perhaps, forgotten.

Not everyone wore their struggles visibly. A good number of people—likely far too many—were experiencing losses and difficulties that they hid from the world. This was a small way he could bring joy to others, and the idea excited him.

He felt a little surprised, but as he dropped the letter to Edith into the mail slot, something warm filled him. This might be a way to be able to help Edith and those she cared about and give her a little bit better of a Christmas. He could hardly wait.

And, if he was being perfectly honest with himself, it might also bring a smile to her face, which was something he loved to do. Even if Edith would never know he was

Santa, he didn't care. He knew he'd lost any chance at affection from her, but he could do this, and he'd feel that connection with her from afar. If that was all he could ever have with her after all of his colossal mistakes, he'd try to be content.

Chapter 9

"You got something in the mail," Mrs. Hedder said, as she motioned her head toward a side table.

Edith flipped through the small bundle o letters until she found the one with her name. Curious, she turned it over and over, looking for the name of the sender. There was none. The handwriting wasn't familiar either.

She tucked it into her pocket and promptly forgot about it until she was changing for bed. Her tiredness gone in an instant when her hand brushed against the paper, Edith opened the envelope and gasped. It was from Santa!

Moving closer to the candle, Edith slowly read each word.

Ms. Clarkson, your letter has been received. Let me see what I can do. But you neglected to mention...what do you want for Christmas?

Santa

Edith hugged the letter to her chest. She had an answer! Then, just as suddenly, she looked at it and frowned. There was no Santa. Not really. Santa was always someone kind, wanting to help others, even if he did have a historical origin. So, who was the mysterious letter sender?

Her eyes traced each letter written on the page. She didn't recognize the handwriting. Still, it didn't change the fact she was holding the letter. Giddiness filled her, as well as delight that she'd gotten a letter from *Santa*.

What should she do now? Edith read the three short lines a few more times, then folded the letter and gently set it on her small table. There was only one thing to do. Keep it a secret. How could Santa have written her back? It didn't appear to be a trick of some kind, but likely someone had received her letter by mistake and thought they'd have a bit of fun writing her back. That was the only reasonable explanation.

Regardless, she'd enjoy that small thrill of Christmas magic, and the letter from "Santa." It didn't matter to her there would be no answer from the man in the red suit himself. She also wouldn't depend on that individual who had written to make her friends' Christmas wishes come true.

She would do it herself. After work tomorrow would be the Christmas party. It was always held early, presumably so the employees could have their Christmas bonus in time to do their Christmas gift buying.

A small smile formed on Edith's face. Even though she had only been at the bank for two Decembers, it had never escaped her notice how kind George was.

"George," Edith whispered.

That smile came again, and Edith tried to push it away. Think of something other than his handsome face, the way his eyes always met hers when they said goodbye. The remorseful and earnest way he'd spoken to her when he'd apologized.

He had mentioned that much of what he said always came out wrong. The very idea of that made her laugh. Surely, he was jesting. A man such as him, a wealthy man, the owner of a bank, always looking confident...surely, he never stumbled over his tongue like an ordinary person. She couldn't recall him doing it often before he'd opened the bank. So, why now?

But she'd believed him. For a moment, something on his face had shone through. It was as though Edith were getting a glimpse of the real George. Someone who was vulnerable, and not quite as assured of himself as he always seemed.

Edith sat at her chair, and looked out her window for a long moment, lost in thoughts of George. She liked working with him. Liked that she felt easy around him again.

Now, if only she could figure out what to do for her friends. There was George's gift too, though his was too important to entrust its care to anyone but herself to its care.

Fabric, along with a needle and thread, sat on the small table, reminding Edith there was work to do. She glanced down and tapped the letter from Santa thoughtfully. Should she answer?

There was nothing to answer, she decided, and picked up the fabric. An hour later, when her eyes were so heavy she kept nodding off, Edith dropped the piece on the table and stumbled into her bed. Morning came too soon, but she got up and ready for her day at work.

The day dragged on, likely because she was excited for the Christmas party. Once the doors were closed and the last customer gone, a small trio of violins set up in the corner of the lobby and played festive favorites. A few of the employees and their spouses danced around the lobby, while others headed to the large table where food had been brought in, all paid for by the bank.

Edith scanned the room. She saw everyone but George. He was often that way, standing at the edges of the crowd. She'd never really thought too much about that until now. When she finally spotted him near the staircase, Edith took a moment to observe him.

He was watching, a slight frown on his face. It eased slightly as he gave a small nod. It was then Edith realized he was making sure everything was going well. The gesture repeated as he studied the musicians, the dancers, and the food. She crossed the room to him.

"It's a lovely party," Edith said.

"It is. Everything looks just as it should," he agreed.

It was true. From greenery around the windows, wreaths on the doors and walls, ribbons and bows on the food table, and a small tree in the corner of the lobby, everything looked perfect.

Edith observed him, then carefully asked, "Why do you always keep to yourself at events like this?"

His shoulders tensed, and he looked at her, the corners of his mouth tight. "I...that is..."

"You deserve to enjoy this as much as anyone else," Edith told him. "After all, you are the one who provided it all."

"Well, yes," he admitted, his brow furrowed, "but this is a gift for you all. And..."

"And?" she asked, when he didn't finish the sentence.

"And I think everyone would rather I not join in. It might keep them from their enjoyment," he answered, not meeting her eyes.

Edith put her hands on her hips. "That's not true. Why, don't you think that way. We're all very grateful to you because you are a generous employer." Her voice quieted. "You are also a good friend to me, and I want others to have your friendship as well."

She then pointed to the food. "Go make a plate and say hello to some of the others. Show them that you aren't just going to stare all evening, but make them—and yourself—feel comfortable by saying hello."

Her bossy tone surprised her, and it seemed to surprise him as well, but George went toward the table, looked back at her, and then took a plate. As he filled it, he seemed to be starting a conversation with Freddy. Soon, the two were smiling and laughing.

Seeing that brought a smile to Edith's face. She couldn't recall seeing him laugh at work before, and it lit his face up in a way that made her stomach all bubbly inside. It was a wonder he wasn't married yet, but Edith wouldn't complain.

Even though it couldn't ever be, as long as he stayed single, there was just a tiny bit of hope that one day he'd show an interest in her. Until then, she'd be happy with what she had. Simply admiring him from afar.

Chapter 10

George stopped to shake out his shoe. Icy crystals tumbled onto the sidewalk where they belonged. Though the snow had been cleared to the sides, he'd been forced to step into an ankle-deep mound in order to let a mother and her child's stroller pass by more easily.

There wasn't much further to walk, though, and then he'd be back at work where he could change into dry socks if these felt too uncomfortable.

The stagecoach office loomed ahead. It was a large building, as a stage came in a minimum of four times a day. They had so many visitors, he expected it wouldn't be long before the railway expanded.

George waited for a carriage to pass before he crossed the street. A woman hurried past, and for a moment he thought it was Edith. He turned to greet her, but saw he was mistaken.

Edith. She'd been on his mind all night long. He'd chuckled each time he thought about how Edith had scolded him at the Christmas party. Yet, her insistence he join in the party made him feel a little bit more welcome in his own bank.

He was also glad of it because it gave him the opportunity to speak with Freddy, who he found out did carpentry on the side and would be able to finish the repairs that needed to be done on his house. George had been more than eager to offer him the job, especially after Freddy had made mention of some of the projects he'd done in the town.

Freddy was a good person. He was conscientious and paid attention to detail in the bank, so George felt confident the man would be the same with the repairs. Additionally, if Freddy were to try and be dishonest, which George was sure he wouldn't be, George knew where he worked. That set him at ease, and he realized that having a relationship with someone on multiple levels really was good for both parties.

George waited in the short line, then stepped up to the ticket window.

"Good morning, Mr. Alcott," the stage manager said. "Going somewhere?"

"No, not me, but I am getting some tickets as a gift." He studied the route on the map tacked to the wall. "Can you get me a ticket that leaves on Christmas Eve and arrives at Midway the same day? I'll also need return fare for a week later."

"Sure can," the manager said. He pulled out a ticket and started to put the information on it. "Want it blank or add a name?"

It occurred to George that he didn't know Mrs. Hedder's first name. "Blank is fine," he said, and set the fare down on the counter.

As the stage manager handed George the tickets, it was hard to stop the smile on his face as he put them in an inside pocket of his overcoat and strode toward the post office.

George had written a letter that morning. He had labored over each word, but in the end, decided that a simple note was best. It was difficult to write in a way that Edith wouldn't recognize, so the less he wrote the easier it was. He also made sure to include the question that burned in him most.

George stopped and read the letter once more.

Dear Ms. Clarkson,

I am enclosing stagecoach tickets for Mrs. Hedder. I will admit, I don't recall ever fulfilling a gift request like this, and it brings me pleasure to know that she will be with her family at Christmas. My best wishes are also enclosed, for the health and recovery of her son.

But, you have not told me yet. What do you want for Christmas?

Santa

He couldn't help but feel excited as he handed the letter—tickets securely inside—to the woman working at the post office. Once assured it would be delivered by tomorrow, he walked to the bank. George couldn't recall the last time he'd bought a surprise for someone, let alone someone who he didn't know. It filled him with a delightfully warm and joyous feeling, and he found he was humming. The spirit of Christmas. That was the only way he could describe that feeling.

It had been far too long since he'd felt such a thing. George decided that next year, he'd figure out a way to play Santa again.

He wished he could see this Mrs. Hedder's face. He also wished he could see Edith's expression when she opened the letter. He hoped she'd be surprised. It was certain that she would be. He had to keep it secret, though, no matter how much he wanted to know how she reacted. If others found out what he was doing, they might suspect him of having an ulterior motive. He didn't want that at all. There was none. Unless you counted just wanting to help.

This peaceful yet excited feeling that filled him right now was just a nice surprise. He hoped it wouldn't be in a hurry to leave. George could get used to feeling this way.

The day passed by slowly for him, and he stole as many glances at Edith as he thought he could risk. When the day ended and he told her goodbye, their gazes lingered a little longer than usual, and all the way home he felt as light as the air.

It was just too bad he couldn't act on these feelings.

Chapter 11

Edith walked through the boarding house door and was surprised to note an envelope with her name on it. Her pulse quickened as she realized the handwriting was the same as before in the letter from...well, it sounded silly, even to her own ears to say it, but, Santa.

She hurried to her room, set the letter down on the table, and looked at it for a full minute before she picked it back up and opened the envelope. As she pulled forth the letter, something fell onto the table. Edith glanced down, and could hardly believe what she saw. Stagecoach tickets!

She read the short letter, then read it again. Tears filled her eyes, and she wiped them away, then lowered her head to say a prayer of thanks. It was unimaginable. Stage tickets. Mrs. Hedder would be overjoyed.

Edith jumped up, and ran down the stairs, and headed to the kitchen—the most likely place to find the boarding house owner this time of day. She was right. Mrs. Hedder was sitting at the table, enjoying a cup of tea.

She glanced up as Edith rushed in. "My word! Is everything all right? You look like something has happened."

"It has!" Edith gasped. She sat down at the table, and with trembling fingers pulled out the tickets, showing Mrs. Hedder. "I wrote Santa and...well, look!"

Mrs. Hedder shook her head as she turned the tickets over in her hands. "I don't understand, dear. What is this?"

"I asked for a way to help you get to your son," Edith explained.

Mrs. Hedder's face turned ashen, then she choked out, "You mean these are for me?"

"Yes," Edith said. "From Santa."

The older woman shook her head. "I don't believe it. I don't."

Edith handed her the letter and watched in pleasure as the older woman read it, her expression one of shock and her eyes misty. "It's true. Someone is playing at being Santa."

"And I will always be grateful to them," Mrs. Hedder said, her voice wobbling as she set the letter down. "Now I can see my boy. Perhaps convince him to move here."

Edith squeezed her hand. "I hope he will," she said softly.

Mrs. Hedder took in a shuddering breath. "You must thank him. Tell him it means the world to this old woman. That I..." She wiped away tears. After a moment, she said, "That I am overcome with joy and gratitude."

"I will," Edith said. She stood from the table. "I'm going to write him right now."

"Are you going to tell him what you want?" Mrs. Hedder asked, curiosity in her voice. "I see he's asked that."

"I just want my friends to have a good Christmas," Edith said over her shoulder. "If you, Mr. Rockingham, and Widow Larson have what you are hoping for, then that's good enough for me."

She meant each word. The joy she had right now for Mrs. Hedder surpassed anything she'd ever felt. She just hoped she'd be able to convey that to Santa so he could also experience a small measure of that happiness.

Edith walked back up the stairs, slower this time. She needed to answer Santa. Thank him properly. But...who was he?

Her mind sorted through the people who she knew might have the means to do something like that for her and Mrs. Hedder. She really didn't know anyone personally. Whoever it was must be well off, and also very good at keeping secrets. For just a moment, she wondered if it was George, but then just as quickly dismissed the idea. She'd recognize his handwriting anywhere. She saw it most every day. The letters were not from him. Besides, he had no idea what she'd asked Santa for. She hadn't told him.

However, Edith did wish she knew who it was. She'd like to thank them in person. As she couldn't, Edith did the next best thing. She pulled out paper, took up her pencil, and wrote, hoping her gratitude would show through her words.

Dear Santa,

I hardly know what to say. There are no words adequate enough to express my surprise at your letter. Your kindness for Mrs. Hedder was overwhelming. You brought her to tears. I don't think anyone has ever done such a kind and wonderful thing for her before. Nor would she expect that. Mrs. Hedder is always the one giving to others. Your gift will be something she talks about the rest of her life.

She sends her gratitude. In fact, her exact words were: "Tell him it means the world to this old woman. That I am overcome with joy and gratitude."

It is true. She could scarcely speak! The expression on her face! Oh, I do wish you could have seen it! She has so much joy within her right now. I suspect, as I write these words, that at this very moment she is writing to her son. I cannot tell you what the chance to see him means to her. He is her only child, and she's worried so much about him.

I wish I knew who you were. Who you really were. Then I could thank you in person. Take your hand and shake it in appreciation. She is so grateful. As am I. I wish to thank you on my behalf, as well. I work for a very generous man at the bank. He even gives us a Christmas bonus. It wasn't going to be enough to get gifts for each of my friends, but with Mrs. Hedder cared for, now I can go about surprising Widow Larson and Mr. Rockingham!

Your gift was truly appreciated, and I must confess, it has brought back a measure of the joy that was missing for me this year. I am eternally grateful to you, Santa, and I hope that you have someone being so kind to you.

I could go on and on, thanking you endlessly, for that is what you deserve, but I'm afraid I have piecework to do for the dressmaker. When I lose myself in work, the things that bother me distract me less. While I don't expect you to have many concerns or worries, you being Santa and all, I expect somehow you understand.

Kind regards,

Edith

She reread the letter, then nodded. That would do. It was a poor thank you for such a momentous gesture, but it would do.

As she put the letter into the envelope, Edith froze. What if whoever it was sending the letters didn't get it? After all, she'd addressed it to Santa, North Pole. She bit her lip in worry. If only she had someone to help her be sure she was doing the right thing to get her letter of thanks to the proper person.

A thought came to mind just then. As soon as it did, she dismissed it. But then it circled around again. George was well connected. He also knew that she'd written to Santa. Surely, he wouldn't laugh at her if she explained her predicament. Perhaps he would know what to do.

Edith sewed for an hour, then made her way to bed. When she closed her eyes, she fell into a peaceful sleep, something that she'd not had for months.

Once morning came, she hurried to the bank, hoping to catch George early, and ask her question in privacy. However, customers were crowded outside of the closed doors when she arrived, and George opened the bank a few moments early. As she helped customer after customer, Edith darted glances at the stairs. Hopefully she'd get a moment alone to talk with him.

Things calmed, and soon it was a few minutes before lunchtime. Edith looked over at Susan. "Would you mind if I went upstairs for a few moments? I need to talk with George."

The other woman nodded. "What do you need him for?"

The woman was the bank gossip, so Edith was careful in her response. "I need to update him on something that got posted a few days ago."

"Oh." Susan turned away, obviously uninterested.

A moment later, Edith held her breath as she knocked on the door.

"Come in," George called.

When Edith pushed open the door, she saw him with a large book before him, and his fingers trailing a row of columns. He looked up, and then smiled. "Hello."

"Hello," Edith said. Her cheeks colored, and she wasn't sure why. Shyness overcame her, and her words got stuck in her throat. Was it that she was about to ask him something that had the potential to embarrass her yet again? Or was it that his warm eyes were so focused on her, Edith felt like she was having trouble breathing?

She was aware that time had passed, more than what was proper for her to be standing there silently. "Ah, I had a question," Edith said finally.

"Of course. How is it that I can help?" George asked, giving her his full attention.

Edith's cheeks burned even hotter. "It's about," she stepped closer and dropped her voice, "that letter I told you I'd written."

"Your letter?" He lowered his voice as well. "To Santa?"

"Yes." Edith straightened. Then she thrust an envelope toward him. "I know it sounds foolish. But I got a reply."

"Oh?" His eyebrows rose.

Edith bobbed her head. "Yes. Read it! And, well, I can hardly believe it, but whoever it was who sent me this letter also enclosed the most wonderful gift for a friend." Edith took a deep breath. "I wrote a thank you. But then I realized something." She bit her lip as she wondered how to ask.

"What did you realize?" George asked. He opened the letter from Santa, read it, and handed it back to her with a smile. "This looks legitimate."

"The man may not be Santa," Edith said. "I doubt that he is. If it is even a he. But whoever the person is, they are very kind." She pulled forth the letter she'd written. "My problem is that I don't know how to get them this thank you. You see, if I simply take it to the post office, well...I'm worried it won't reach the person it needs to go to."

George nodded seriously. "May I?" he asked and held out his hand.

With a nod, Edith handed him her letter. Their fingers brushed, just like they had when he'd handed her the stack of mail a few days ago. She sucked in a breath, and could have sworn he did the same.

George's hand had frozen, his fingers touching hers. Edith glanced at him under her lowered lashes. His expression was one of uncertainty, but also something else she couldn't decipher. Almost reluctantly, he pulled the letter toward him, and Edith lowered her hand.

He looked at the envelope addressed to Santa thoughtfully. "If you trust me, I will be sure it gets into the right hands."

"Then you know who wrote it?" Edith gasped. She clasped her hands and brought them close to her chest. "Who is it?"

He hesitated, then answered wryly, "I think, had they wished to be known, they'd have not written as Santa. You wish me to divulge someone's Christmas secret?"

She laughed. "You are right. Forgive me. I won't try to pry the secret from you. But, if you can't get the letter to them, you'll let me know?"

"I will," he promised. "Though I feel certain I can have it delivered today."

Her smile was so big it was hurting her cheeks. She had been right to come to him. "Thank you," she said. "Let me know how I can repay you."

"Seeing your smile is thanks enough," George told her. He hesitated, then offered, "Are you sure I can't do something more for you? Perhaps a loan from me to you?"

Edith shook her head. "No," she answered firmly. "With Santa, whoever they may be, being so generous, and my extra job, I feel sure I can help my friends. Perhaps not in the way they want, but in a way that will still please them."

He searched her face in a way that almost made her squirm. Edith knew her cheeks must be red again under his scrutiny. "You are working too hard," he said, a hint of worry in his tone.

"I enjoy it," Edith said. "To help another brings me joy." Her voice grew soft. "And it helps me not feel lonely this time of year."

George swallowed so hard she could see his Adam's apple. He nodded, looked down at her letter, and then glanced back up at her. "I understand those feelings," he said quietly. "I will see your letter safe to where it needs to be. On one condition."

It was her turn to raise her eyebrows. "What would that be?"

"That you promise to always tell me if there is something I can do to help you," he said, his eyes nearly piercing through her.

"I will," Edith said. And then, reacting without thinking, she reached over and rested her hand on his. "Thank you," she said, pulling it away and then turning to the door.

Edith didn't look backward. She didn't dare. As she closed the door behind her, she leaned against the wall for a moment, trying to slow the racing of her heart.

"I must be careful," she whispered to herself. Straightening, Edith walked shakily to collect her lunch.

She must be careful indeed. It would be far too easy to fall back in love with George. And once she gave him her heart again, she knew she'd never love another.

Chapter 12

George watched Edith leave his office. He felt the responsibility of the letter she had entrusted him with. He could hardly believe that she had approached him. It made him feel both proud and hopeful that their past misunderstanding—because of his stupidity—was behind them now.

He could not wait to read the letter she had written to Santa. After a moment had passed and he was certain that no one would come into his office, he pulled the letter free from the envelope. This time, there was no hesitation. After all, the letter was meant for him.

A smile formed as he read. So much happiness filled him at her words upon the page. He could almost envision Edith writing them, see her expressions as she labored over each sentence in her retelling.

Even though he had never met Mrs. Hedder, he could almost imagine the older woman's response to the gift of the stagecoach tickets. The thanks the boarding house owner passed along made him feel warm inside.

George reread the letter and then reflected on how fortunate he was in his life. If he'd needed to travel for a loved one's care, he'd easily have the means, and simply could just buy the tickets. Not everyone could. It was something that he knew, something he was keenly aware of—the fact that others were less fortunate than he was.

Yet, he admitted to himself, perhaps he was not always as aware of that as he could be, likely because of his always keeping that emotional distance between himself and others. For so many years, he'd kept that distance. It was only now he was seeing how much he missed because of it.

He hadn't known about Freddy needing to take on extra work, just like he hadn't known Edith had. If he missed such an obvious thing about his friend, how much more was he missing about his employees? Or acquaintances? It could be that with very little effort on his part, he could have helped others. Made their lives easier.

George straightened in his chair, a determined expression on his face. It was too late to change the past. There was nothing he could do there. But the future. That he could.

The next matter of business, George knew, would be the shawl for Widow Larson. While he had never gone shopping for a woman's shawl, he was certain that Jake's wife, Louise, would be able to help him find exactly what Widow Larson was hoping for.

Fortunately, there was still time to order such a thing to be custom made if they didn't have one in the store. George decided to go that afternoon after work to make the purchase. Then he remembered.

He had a dinner engagement.

It was not something he was looking forward to in the least. However, Jake had begged the favor for him to entertain a friend from out of town. He said Louise had a prior event that evening, and Jake, being a married man, couldn't very well dine alone with her. He also had to stay with the children.

She was a single woman, and George had the suspicion that Jake was trying to be helpful and set him up with her. He wasn't the least bit interested. However, seeing as he had been asked just a few hours before, and told the woman would be waiting, it would have been a rude of him to call off the meal and put her in an uncomfortable position. Thankfully, the woman seemed to be just passing through, so he didn't have to worry too much about entertaining her in the future.

He hoped. He also hoped Jake wouldn't do something like this again. Maybe he should have told his friend he was interested in Edith.

Of course, there was always the chance that he and this woman would actually make some sort of connection. George told himself he should be open to the possibility and accept whatever came, since he had no attachment, and no prospects of one either. However, he knew deep in his heart, the only person who he wanted any sort of relationship with was Edith.

But would she want the same? Twice now recently, their fingers had brushed against each other. It had filled him with such an electric surge, George thought it must be impossible for Edith not to feel the same. He'd tried to steal a glance at her, see if she'd noticed, but he'd been unable to tell.

The workday passed quickly, and every time George looked at Edith, happiness shone on her face. He was sure it was because of the gift for her friend, and it made him happy that he had been able to do that for her.

Seeing her happiness made him realize now that the Edith had always smiled and been kind and gracious to everyone who crossed her path, even if the last year or so there had been a lingering sadness in her face. Today, he did not see that. It was something that he did not want to ever see again.

George touched the pocket where her letter lay. Once again, Edith did not tell George what she wanted for Christmas. He fully intended to make sure that each of her friends had just what they wanted, but he also wanted to give Edith something extra special.

The question of what had played on his mind much of the afternoon. He didn't want to give her just anything. Knowing his luck, he'd accidentally get something that upset her, but as she was not telling him at all what she would like, it was making the situation nearly impossible to figure out.

As if she sensed him watching, Edith's eyes found his, and she smiled. Flustered, George pretended to straighten a picture on the wall. He could tell, though, by the amusement on her face, she knew he'd been caught staring.

George gave her a grin and a small shrug, then turned as a bank customer approached him. It wasn't just Edith who had changed since Santa had written. More good had come of her writing to Santa than simply the gift for Mrs. Hedder. Until Jake had said something, George realized that though he had always tried to be friendly to his employees, by keeping himself at such a distance he had not fully been aware of many of the hardships happening.

If one was to be a good business owner or boss, they needed to know more about those who worked for them, and how they could support them so that they might perform the best job possible.

For example, about Edith. And how she was struggling after the loss of her mother because she had given her nest egg to care for her mother, and now she was left with almost nothing. He had become more observant in the last few days, and learned that Susan Cooper had a husband with a very bad back. Sometimes he would go months without being able to work. Often, hers was the only income they had.

And then there was Freddy. He worked two jobs to care for his aging in-laws as well as his growing family. Freddy did not once complain, and his work was superb. George was more than pleased with it so far. But this newfound knowledge made him realize that he was not only robbing himself of the opportunity to get to know his employees, but also to offer a sympathetic ear if nothing else.

There was so much he had been missing in the lives of others he should have been familiar with. If only he had realized that sooner. Edith's words in her letter to him about working so much so that she would forget about things had resonated with him. Was that maybe why he did the same? Why he would bring home work or stay late at the office? Really, how often did some of the things he did have to be done?

Perhaps it was all just an excuse to stave away the constant companion of loneliness once he got home.

The day was finally over, and George reluctantly said goodbye to each of the employees as they left. He wasn't in a hurry for his dinner date or to have Edith away from him.

"Have a good evening, Edith," he said as she approached the door.

"Thank you," she replied.

They locked eyes for just a moment. George would have loved to say something more, to take just a minute to gaze at her beautiful face. But there was someone behind Edith. She stepped forward, then turned to gaze at him before raising her hand in farewell and walking away. George felt that unwelcome hollow within him and wondered if it would ever go away.

Once he had locked the bank, he checked the time and then headed over to the small restaurant Jake had asked him to meet his friend at. Her name was Florence. That was all he knew about her. However, the moment George appeared, he knew it was not going to be a good meal.

As he walked to the front of the restaurant, a woman wearing entirely too much perfume asked, "Are you George?" At his nod, she answered, "I'm Florence. Your date for the evening." She giggled, and before he could answer, she had looped her arm through his and practically dragged him into the restaurant.

They were seated shortly, and Florence surveyed the menu set before her.

"Do you need a few moments?" the waiter asked.

"Not at all," Florence answered. "I'll have the most expensive thing on the menu." She giggled again and fluttered her eyelashes. "After all, Mr. Alcott can more than afford to pay. He owns a bank."

George stiffened. He smiled politely and reminded himself he was doing this for Jake. Jake, who was now going to owe him a very large favor.

"I'll take the meatloaf," he answered, and the waiter walked away.

The food was the only good thing the entire dinner. Florence chattered nonstop about herself, the places that she had been, and what she liked to buy. And she left more than a few suggestions about where she would like to go on their next outing.

George was glad when the polite number of minutes had passed at the end of their meal, and he was able to stand up and walk her outside.

"It's been a lovely evening," he said. "Be sure to tell Jake I'll be calling on him soon."

He saw Florence into a carriage and quickly walked away before she could say anything else.

How was it that two women could be such complete contrasts, he wondered. Florence, who immediately didn't even try to make a good impression but simply ordered the most expensive thing on the menu because she thought he could afford it, and Edith, who wouldn't even think about what she wanted as a Christmas gift for herself.

Edith was nothing if not selfless. And George realized that she had been on his mind nonstop. He wasn't sure how he could think about anyone else or if he even wanted to. It was important that he did, though, because falling in love with Edith would lead to nothing but heartache when she ended up finding someone else. Someone who was brave enough to confess his affection. The kind of person who she truly deserved. Not someone like him. Withholding his true feelings because he was scared to let anyone inside. Even the woman that he knew he could love. Did love.

Chapter 13

"Thank you for helping me bake all these cookies," Mrs. Hedder said. "And to think that you also helped with the decorating of the house for Christmas. I don't know where you find all your energy, Edith. I know how hard you work both at the bank and at night for the dressmaker."

Mrs. Hedder shook her head as she pulled another pan of cookies from the oven. "I'm still very grateful for it, though. Never had a daughter, but I suspect if I did she would be just like you. At least, I hope she would be."

Edith smiled with pleasure. "I'm happy to help you anytime. And as for where I get the energy? Well, I don't know. I suppose that's just another bit of Christmas magic helping me."

Edith used the heavy wooden spoon to stir the batter in the bowl. "This gingerbread is going to be wonderful once it's finished. My mouth is already watering."

"It's my favorite thing to give as gifts," Mrs. Hedder admitted. "I enjoy making it, and others enjoy eating it."

"Speaking about gifts," Edith said, "I was thinking I would like to make George some sort of a gift. At the bank, we employees were talking among ourselves, but no one could quite agree on what to get him for Christmas. Everything they suggested sounded just so impersonal. There was no thought behind any of it. It was all something like prepaying for a meal at a restaurant or a set of new ledger books."

"That does sound dull," the boarding house owner agreed.

"Nothing had any thought behind it," Edith said. "We all decided just to simply make something small ourselves. I'd planned to do that anyway, honestly. I always give him something. I think Mrs. Cooper is going to give him some of the jam that she had put up over the summer. Just I'm not sure what I could make."

"Well, you are very talented with your knitting," Mrs. Hedder said. "What about a scarf? You can't go wrong with a nice warm scarf. It's just the right level of personal for a friend or boss. A gift that they would use, but also practical."

"Hmm," Edith mused.

Mrs. Hedder went on. "It's nothing too intimate as to make anyone feel awkward, while still a gift that shows you took time and care to make it."

"Oh, that's a wonderful idea," Edith answered. "I think I'll do just that. I'll go down to the general store here in a little bit and find some yarn. Thank you, Mrs. Hedder. You have the most wonderful of ideas."

"I won't lie," Mrs. Hedder said. "I'm feeling the Christmas spirit this year. The thought that I'll get to go and see my boy and spend a whole week with him—at Christmas no less—has filled me with such happiness. I'm refusing to even worry about what you all will do here at the boarding house."

"And you shouldn't worry," Edith said. "We will take care of ourselves. You go and have a wonderful time. We expect nothing less."

A short time later, Edith found herself outside of the general store. She paused for a moment to admire the shop window. While she didn't know the owners very well, as she had only gone in a few times, they seemed very nice. Louise was quite talented at dressing the shop window. She changed it every week.

Today, paper snowflakes hung upon thin wire from the ceiling, and white fabric spread below represented snow. A child's sled rested on top of the ersatz snow, with a row of teddy bears sitting upon it. Opposite sat a ball and some books and a few other children's toys.

She took a moment to gaze at the scene, and let herself drift to the past. Memories of her own childhood, and when she eagerly anticipated Christmas and the gift Santa would bring, filled her. How incredible it had been already this year to have a special gift from him.

Edith pushed the shop door open. Hopefully, she'd find the perfect yarn for making George a gift. Last year, she'd gotten him a novel. The year before, a pen. She'd noticed it was on his desk at work. So that meant he must like her gifts.

"Welcome," Louise said.

Edith returned the greeting, and headed right to where there was a large display of yarn. She felt the softness of several skeins and then frowned. What color would be the best? There were so many to choose from, everything from shades of blue and green to a nice burgundy, a wheat color and, of course, varying shades of white and cream.

Uncertain, her fingers went from color to color. Edith had her hand on a dark blue when someone stood next to her. Without looking in their direction, she moved her hand to step out of the way so the person could also look at the yarn, when she realized who was standing right next to her.

"George," Edith said in surprise.

"Hello," he told her with a smile on his face. "I didn't expect to see you here. Doing some knitting?"

"Yes," she told him. "I wanted to make a gift for someone." Then she asked, "It's hard to choose a color. What do you think? If something were made for you, what color would you enjoy?"

He studied the choices in front of him seriously, and then reached out and handed her a moss-colored green. "This one," he said, "because during the bleakest winter days, a beautiful green reminds you of spring and new growth and warm summer days, soft moss alongside a trickling bank that you're lying next to reading or enjoying a picnic."

Edith stared at him in surprise. "That was beautifully said."

George laughed and shook his head. "I guess you can tell how much I enjoy the warmer weather."

"I do as well. Do you remember some of those picnics we had years ago? I always enjoyed them." Edith took the yarn from his hands. "What you said sounds lovely, especially on this chilly day, and I think that this color will be just perfect."

"I'm glad I could be of help," George answered.

Their eyes locked once more. And Edith couldn't help but feel nervous. There was a tension in the air again, but not in a bad way. It was that kind of feel where she wanted to draw closer. Perhaps even had. Their eyes were locked, and Edith shivered, but it wasn't due to the draft from the nearby window.

"Did you find what you needed?" Louise asked, coming up behind them so quietly, Edith hadn't heard her.

Edith whirled around. "Yes. Yes, I did." She followed Louise to the front counter, but looked over her shoulder. "Thank you again, George. See you later?"

He nodded, and Edith felt his eyes on her as she paid and left. If only Louise hadn't interrupted that moment between them. Who knows what might have happened? This was a time of Christmas miracles, wasn't it? Perhaps just a little tiny bit of that Christmas magic would make something special happen for her.

Chapter 14

George watched as Edith left the general store. He felt both glad she hadn't spotted him with a shawl in hand and curious just who she was knitting something for. She had so little time, whoever they were was special indeed. A tiny flash of concern flickered through him then. It wasn't quite jealousy, but something akin to it.

Who was going to be the gift's recipient? She wouldn't have seemed so concerned over the color if it was just for anyone. That meant the gift was for someone special. Was it...a beau?

George swallowed hard, hoping it wasn't. He didn't think she had one, but admittedly, he now rarely saw Edith outside of the bank. That environment didn't lend itself to much personal conversation, such as the events of one's weekends or evenings. Best to take his mind off the situation, and do what he'd set out to do.

He dug into his pocket and pulled out the letter from Edith. A shawl with red roses on it.

"Are you looking for anything in particular?" Louise asked, coming over to him.

"I am," George said. "A gift for someone. She wants a shawl with red roses on it. Would you happen to have such a thing?"

Louise nodded. "I do. It was in the store window a few weeks back, but no one has bought it yet. Let me go and get it for you. I moved it when I did this new display."

George nodded and waited while Louise went and retrieved the shawl. She unfolded it, and held it up for him to see. "That looks good," he said, though he didn't really know much about women's fashion. It was a soft gray color, with red roses along the trim. "Would you wrap it and deliver it for me?"

"Of course," she assured him. "I would be glad to."

"I'd like to include a note," George said.

"I will get you some paper," Louise said. She turned away and a moment later set some before him, along with the stub of a pencil.

Children's footsteps sounded, and Louise rushed away to prevent a display being knocked over. "Ellie and Phil," she scolded. The sound of her voice faded away as she led the children to another part of the store.

George leaned overtop the sheet, unsure what to enclose. He had to have a note, but wanted to keep it short. Finally, he wrote:

Dear Ms. Clarkson,

I have sent you a shawl with red roses for Widow Larson. I hope she will like it. But you still have not told me. What do you want for Christmas?

Santa

Louise came back toward him, and George hastily folded the note. "When can you get this delivered?" he asked.

"Is it here in town?" Louise asked as she measured out brown paper and started to bundle the shawl.

"To the boarding house," George said.

Louise glanced down to the name he'd written. "Wasn't that the young lady who was just here?"

"Yes, though it isn't for her. I'm just playing Santa," George told her with a wink and a finger over his lips. "I'd appreciate your confidence."

"Of course." Louise smiled. "It will be this evening, after the store closes. Jake will drop it off. Is there anything else I can help you find?"

"I hope so," George said. "I need one more gift. I don't know much more than he is a man who is lonely. I'm not sure what to get him."

"That is difficult," Louise agreed. "A book doesn't last long, and likely the man is tired of reading and his own company." She tapped her cheek in thought.

George nodded. "That's where I'm stuck."

"I'll keep thinking," Louise promised. Then she added, as Jake walked in, "How did your evening with Florence go?"

George scowled at Jake. "You owe me," he said.

"Was it that bad?" Jake asked, his face one of innocence. "I thought the two of you might hit it off."

"How could you think that?" George gaped. "She was not anything like the type of woman I'd like."

Jake shrugged and grinned. "Then why not ask out the one you want? And stop being so shy?"

Sputtering, George said, "I don't know what you are talking about."

"Of course not," Jake chuckled. Louise walked away to greet a customer, and Jake tapped the package addressed to Edith. His finger stopped on her name, and his eyes held mischief. "Should I pass along any message when I drop this off to her?"

George stiffened. "The contents aren't for Edith, but a friend of hers. I'd appreciate you not mentioning who sent the package."

"He's playing at Santa," Louise explained as she walked past them, picked up a catalog, and scurried back to the customer. "So don't you dare tell a soul, Jake, or I'll make you biscuits all week," she warned, glancing over her shoulder.

Jake winced and promised, "Your secret is safe with me."

"Biscuits?" George asked curiously.

"More like tooth-breaking cannonballs," Jake explained. "Been there, done that, and thank goodness we own a store with foodstuffs and there are some diners in town."

George laughed, waved, and headed outside. He wished he could see the faces on Edith and Widow Larson when the package arrived, but that was impossible. It would not only look suspicious, but also be strange, as he didn't know Widow Larson at all.

A couple on the street stopped, and the woman adjusted a knit scarf around the man's neck. George felt the small act cut through him, as again he wondered who Edith was knitting for. Was it going to be a scarf? Would she fasten it around some other man's neck? Moving close and letting her hands linger around his collarbone? Maybe he shouldn't have told her the color he liked. If he saw that on someone else, he'd know, and it would be all the worse.

He sighed and turned back the direction he'd come from, then apologized as he bumped into someone. "Edith!" he said a second later, once he realized who it was. "I didn't expect to see you again so soon."

She laughed, "Indeed. Mrs. Hedder, the boarding house owner, asked if I'd take something to the post office. I was just coming back."

"Join me in the bakery for a snack?" he asked hopefully. George held his breath, hoping she'd say yes.

"I would love to," Edith said.

With a wide grin, George held open the door of the bakery, which was conveniently right in front of them. Warmth and the yeasty sweet smell of baked goods struck his nose. Edith was also glancing around, appreciative.

"My treat," George told her and stepped up to the glass case. "What looks good to you?"

"All of it," Edith said. "I've always had a hard time choosing."

"Me too," George said. "Do you want to find us a table while I order?"

She nodded, and as she walked away, George said, pointing at the selections, "A pot of tea please, two of those orange muffins, a strawberry tart, a chocolate cookie, a slice of that cake, and another of that one there."

"I'll bring it all out," the young woman behind the counter said as he paid.

George joined Edith, and a moment later, a tray was set before them. Edith laughed, "So much!"

"It's been too long since we've had a chance to do something like this," George told her. He hesitated,

"That's my fault. I...I guess when you started to work for the bank I..."

"Don't," Edith said and shook her head. "It's not your fault. We've both tried to be careful. After all, neither of us are married, people would talk and, well, you own a bank. The bank I work for. Neither of us wants trouble."

"I didn't want that to ever get in the way of our friendship," George said quietly. "I worry that I have."

"You've not," Edith said firmly. She reached over and took a muffin. "Things just got busy. And then my mother..." She stopped, and that sad expression on her face returned.

"I should have been there more," George said. "For that, I am sorry. I wasn't there the way I should have been. Didn't know how bad things were. How much you suffered," George felt as though his heart was about to burst with sorrow. When he saw Edith, this wasn't the conversation at all he'd intended. But, he couldn't seem to stop it.

Edith set her muffin down and rested her hand on his. He tried to ignore the tingling warmth running through him. "George, the fault is not yours. You are blameless. I never really asked for help. I could have. But I wanted to do things on my own. Handle my grief and worry my own way. The times I did reach out—not to you—I got platitudes. Niceties. Not really any real help. The people I thought might, didn't. And it made me hurt so much."

Edith's voice trembled. "I didn't want to ask anymore. The pain of being ignored or rejected hurt too much. So, I didn't. I just tried to pretend all was well."

"I do that sometimes," George said. He rested his hand on top of hers. "It doesn't always work well, does it?"

She shook her head. "No, it doesn't." Edith smiled at him sadly. "Oh, George. What happened to the children we were? So determined life would go our way?"

He was quiet for a long moment. She was right. It felt so long ago that things were easy. Without expectations and worries. "We lost our way," he told her. "But that doesn't mean that we can't find it again."

Edith smiled, a true smile that warmed him. "You are right. Starting now. This is the season of miracles."

"So you have said." He squeezed her hand gently, then released it.

"So I *know*." Edith leaned forward and whispered. "You are aware Santa has answered one of my letters! How is that not a miracle? An answer to my prayers."

"Do you think he will help with your other wishes?" George asked curiously.

"I don't expect anything more. That itself was tremendous. I will figure something out," Edith said. "Even if it is just something small, I will be sure to bring some happiness to my friends this Christmas."

"You are such a good person," George said, admiring the determination in her tone and on her face. He pushed the plates of treats toward her to encourage Edith to take another. "But what of you? Don't you have a Christmas wish?"

She just smiled. "I do. But that's a secret."

"Is that so?" he asked.

"Yes. And what of you?" she asked George, raising her eyebrows as she dug her fork into the slice of cake.

"Mine is also a secret," he teased.

The air between them lightened, and it was as if no time at all had passed. When the tea and pastries were gone, George walked Edith to the boarding house and watched as she waved from the doorway. The lack of her presence made him feel hollow inside, and George suppressed the sigh that wanted to burst out.

He knew just what he wanted for Christmas. Another chance with Edith. He just wasn't sure if he'd be able to have it.

Chapter 15

Edith sat in the front room of the boarding house. Mr. Rockingham was reading from a book, and she and Widow Larson were listening. Edith was working on the scarf for George while Widow Larson was mending the sleeve on a blouse.

It had been a lovely afternoon. She hadn't expected to run into George again, and their time at the bakery together had felt just like old times. She'd enjoyed just sitting and talking with him, laughing, and sharing her thoughts. Things had gotten serious for a moment, but that wasn't bad. She'd never minded deeper conversations with George. He'd always been someone she could ask anything to.

Though, she wished she'd never asked about the loan. Still, had she not, some kind stranger might never have helped Mrs. Hedder to get that stage ticket. She'd be leaving in a few days, and was overjoyed. It made Edith smile each time she thought about it.

There was a knock at the front door. Mr. Rockingham paused the book. "I'll go," Edith said. "Keep reading."

He nodded, and his words faded behind her as she left the room. The general store owner, Jake, stood waiting at the door. "Evening," he said, and offered her the package. Before she could say anything, he had hurried off, hands jammed deeply into his pockets and his collar turned up against the cold.

Edith quickly shut the door. It was sure to snow more. The air was not only biting, but it was damp. The sun never did more than peek out that entire week. She couldn't wait for the warm days of summer again.

"What have you there?" Mrs. Hedder asked as she walked past.

"I don't know. I didn't order anything," Edith answered.

"Perhaps it's from Santa," Mrs. Hedder answered. "Open it!"

She hesitated a moment, but after a second, Edith did. Carefully, she untied the twine, and then gasped as a beautiful shawl lay before her.

"I'll be," Mrs Hedder whispered. Then she pointed. "There's a note, dear."

Edith's fingers were nearly frozen with shock, and she fumbled to open it, then read aloud.

Dear Ms. Clarkson,

I have sent you a shawl with red roses for Widow Larson. I hope she will like it. But you still have not told me. What do you want for Christmas?

Santa

"In all my years," Mrs. Hedder whispered. She didn't finish her thought, just shook her head, wonder in her eyes. "There is good in this world still. Who'd have thought our little home would be the recipient of some of it?"

"Let's go give it to her," Edith said, her fingers trembling in excitement as she folded the garment.

"When you write him back, will you answer his question?" the older woman asked, holding the letter in her hand.

Edith paused as she wrapped the shawl back into the paper. "I am already getting what I want," she said.

Her friend frowned, and started to argue, but Edith shook her head. "I don't want for anything."

It wasn't true, and they both knew that, but how could Edith even dream of asking for something for herself? Especially after all that this person had done for her?

They went into the parlor. Mr. Rockingham paused his story. "What have you there?" he asked, indicating the parcel.

"Another Christmas miracle," Mrs. Hedder said, tears in her eyes.

Widow Larson looked surprised as Edith handed her the bundle. "This is for you," she told her. "From Santa."

"From Santa?"

They all knew Santa had gifted Mrs. Hedder the tickets, but none of them had expected anything more. Widow Larson's eyes were wide and her fingers trembled as she pulled back the brown paper. Then, she gave a choked sob as she pulled out the shawl.

Widow Larson sprang to her feet, and draped it around herself. With tears rolling down her aged cheeks, she gasped, "Look at me! Look at me!"

Edith found tears falling down her own face as she embraced the other woman. They sprang into her eyes again as she sat down an hour later to write her letter.

Dear Santa,

You have made us all cry tonight with your gift for Widow Larson. While I don't know the full story of it, I think I wrote to you in an earlier letter how years ago, she was coming home one evening and was attacked for whatever money was in her purse. She didn't have much, and had tried to protect it. The thief hurt her badly, and she suffers from scars on her face and arms. They've always embarrassed her. But this shawl...it has brought such happiness to her and made her feel beautiful again. I wish you could have seen her.

Who are you? Santa, you say. But Santa doesn't leave gifts for adults, so I know you must be some sort of a kind stranger. Perhaps even a friend of George, as he promised to get my last letter of thanks to you? I do hope you received it, dearest Santa.

I know you keep asking what I would like for Christmas. What you have done is more than enough. There is nothing more that I want or need than my friends wearing a smile and feeling loved.

Gratefully yours,

Edith

She folded the letter, put it into an envelope, and hardly slept that night. When the sun rose, Edith hurried to the bank, arriving at the same time George was letting himself in.

"George," she whispered urgently.

He frowned. "Is everything okay? You are here earlier than usual."

"It's because I must talk to you," Edith said.

Once the bank door was open and they were in the lobby, she reached into her handbag, fishing about for the letter. "George, you won't believe it."

"What won't I believe?" he asked.

"Santa! He sent Widow Larson a gift," she said. Then, she thrust the letter at him. "Can you...would you get this to him? Santa?"

"I will," George promised. He took the envelope, but then caught her hand in his. "Edith, I want to ask you something."

The air felt charged, much as it had in the general store, and Edith's heart started to hammer. "What is it?" she asked softly.

"All last night I was thinking," he confessed. "About how things used to be. About how I had wanted them to be. And about how I'd made mistakes that prevented them from getting there."

His words were confusing, but Edith knew somehow, they had something to do with the two of them. George had stepped closer, and put the letter in his pocket, and now was holding both of her hands in his.

"Edith, would you...could you give us a—"

Just then, the bank door swung open, and Susan walked inside. George hastily released her hands, a panicked look on his face.

Edith calmly said, "Thank you for posting that for me, George." She turned toward the stairs. "Good morning, Susan! Let me put my handbag and coat down, and then I want to hear about your weekend."

A moment later, she was downstairs, half listening as Susan rambled on about the things she'd done over the weekend while her husband's back healed. All the while, she wondered what George had been about to say, and when he might try to finish it.

If he would. There was a very strong chance that he wouldn't, that he'd have time to rethink or change his mind. The very idea frustrated her, because Edith knew that's how George was. He was always careful, cautious, almost to the point of irritation.

It was a busy day. With only four days until Christmas, she hardly had a moment to catch her breath. Even George was running around, meeting with customers and looking as exhausted as she felt by the time it was the end of the day.

As he stood by the front door, letting everyone leave, Edith tried to linger, hoping he would want to continue their conversation, but Freddy ruined any chance of that.

"George, can we take a fast look at anything else you'd like done?" he asked. "I told my wife I'd be home late, doing the last of your repairs. We both want you snug and settled in before Christmas."

"Oh, er, yes, of course," George stammered, while giving Edith a worried look.

"Go on." She smiled. "But do make sure my letter goes where it needs to?"

"I will," he promised. "Have a good evening, Edith."

She didn't answer, but felt his hand brush against the small of her back. There, the phantom of his fingertips tingled all the way back to the boarding house. She hadn't wasted a moment after dinner, and had set to work immediately upon George's gift. There wasn't much time left to complete it.

Exhausted, Edith closed her eyes for a moment before she resumed her knitting, and let herself imagine what George might have said this morning. Though she didn't know the exact words, she hoped more than anything he'd try again. It had seemed important. Private. Serious, though not in a bad way. Not if he had been holding her hands.

Perhaps if he couldn't tell her how he felt, she'd do it, and accept whatever consequences came. That's all she wanted for Christmas. Another chance with him. There wasn't anyone else who could have a piece of her heart. Edith had saved it entirely for him.

Chapter 16

George was feeling extraordinarily nervous. It was just days before Christmas, and though he had wandered into every single shop in Richmond, he couldn't find a single gift that would be suitable for a man in need of companionship. He had browsed the newspaper and even magazines, looking at the advertisements and hoping he could find the perfect item for Mr. Rockingham, but what did you get a man who is in need of companionship?

He and Louise had agreed that a book was not a good idea. Neither would be a magazine or newspaper subscription. The only thing that came to mind was a mail-order bride, and he wasn't sure that would be a proper solution! Still, he wanted to find something for the man, especially something that would make him happy. It wasn't a good feeling to be lonely; it was something that he knew a great deal about and hoped that he could come across the perfect solution.

There was one more person he also sought a gift for. George decided that in addition to the bonus that he usually gave his housekeeper at Christmastime, he wanted to also give her a small gift to open. So he headed towards Jake's store. When he got there, Louise looked up at him excitedly.

"I was hoping you would stop in or that I would see you pass by," she told him.

"Oh?" George asked.

"Yes. I might have the perfect solution for that final gift that you needed." Her eyes were nearly twinkling.

"Really?" George asked. "For the man who was lonely?"

"That's the one," Louise said. "Come with me. It's in the back storage room."

George followed her through the store, first past the sewing notions and perfumed soaps, then beyond children's toys, books, and farming tools until they came to a closed door.

"Here we are." Louise opened the door.

As he stuck his head in, George saw a wriggling mass of fur in a box in the corner. Several sets of bright eyes stared at him curiously.

"What's this?" he asked as he knelt next to the kittens, who had gone back to their playful antics.

Louise watched from the doorway. "The children found a cat about two months ago. We kept it to help catch mice in the store. However," Louise explained, "we didn't realize that it was a mother cat and she was going to have a litter because that's quite unusual for this time of year."

George nodded in agreement.

"She had her kittens about six weeks ago, and it completely escaped my mind until last night, when Jake mentioned how he hoped we could find homes for these kittens as they would make great companions."

"Companions! Yes," George agreed excitedly. He made sure to keep his voice quiet, so as not to frighten the kittens. "This might be just the perfect thing. May I really have one?"

"Take your pick," Louise told him. "You are welcome to any of them. I've got the most perfect little basket the kitten can be put in. It has a lid with a fastener on it, and we can deliver it for you today."

George studied each of the tiny kittens. It was obvious they were siblings, yet they were still very different from each other. No two looked the same. There were shades of gray and black. Some bore stripes, some patches, and one was solid. There were six kittens in total.

George stroked their little heads and let their small paws wrap around his finger. One kitten, obviously the bravest of them all, stood on its tiny little paws and walked toward him. It was a gray striped kitten and it started to purr and rub against him.

"This one," George said. "He's already got a friendly personality."

"I think that's a perfect choice," Louise agreed. "He's the sweetest one in the whole bunch, the bravest, and I think the one who will most settle easily settle into a new environment. Bring him to the front, and I will go get a basket," she said.

George scooped up the little kitten and nuzzled it close to him. When he turned back to look once more at the litter, the solid black kitten had stepped forward, then sat, watching him.

He followed Louise partway through the store, and then hesitated. "Is it possible to have a second kitten?" he asked.

"Yes, of course. Do you know someone else who would like one?"

George hoped he wasn't too red-faced as he answered, "I would not mind one for myself."

"Go pick one out," she encouraged, "and you can take it with you while we deliver the other one."

George hurried back to the storeroom. The black kitten was waiting for him. George scooped him up and went back to the front. Louise had the gray kitten nestled inside of a small lidded basket with a long handle.

"I put a scrap of cloth on the inside to make it more comfortable for him," she said. Then she offered, "Did you want to write a note to go along with this gift as well?"

"Yes," George said. "This will also go to the boarding house." He took the offered paper and pencil and then put the black kitten inside of his jacket pocket. He could feel it turning around before it settled. There was a soft vibration as it nestled into his pocket.

"I'll give you privacy to write your note," Louise said and disappeared. George thought for a long moment and then painstakingly wrote each letter, trying to mask his handwriting.

Dear Ms. Clarkson,

I hope that this will be a suitable companion for Mr. Rockingham. I also hope that the boarding house owner will excuse my assumption of a pet. I realize belatedly I do not know her guidelines, but this young kitten seems to be a good companion, and I hope it will bring joy to your friend.

However, we draw close to Christmas, and once again you have not told me what it is you want.

Santa

George folded the letter and handed it to Louise. She tucked it inside of the basket. "Jake will deliver this in about half an hour."

"That sounds perfect," George said. "Thank you very much for your help." He started to leave the store when he remembered that he had wanted the gift for his housekeeper and turned right back around.

"Did you need something else?" Louise asked.

"Yes, I almost forgot. I'd originally come in here for one more gift. Something for my housekeeper."

When he left a few moments later with a box of embroidered handkerchiefs and a tin of hard candies, George was feeling rather pleased. Not only had this Christmas turned out to be one where he did end up with several people to buy gifts for, he had done his shopping for all but one person.

Edith.

He wished he knew what it was that she wanted. Part of him had thought of getting her a kitten, but if he had, that would not have made the gift for Mr. Rockingham as special. George hoped that there would be time to hear her reply before Christmas because, if not, well, he wasn't sure what he was going to do for Edith.

The kitten stirred in his pocket, peeking a tiny nose out before snuggling back into the warmth of his coat. George hurried into his home and filled a small bowl with milk for the kitten. The housekeeper was already gone, but dinner waited. Before he ate, he made a bed for the kitten. He'd still not settled upon a name, but was sure one would come to him.

Over the warm potato soup, George reread the letters that Edith had given him for Santa. He couldn't help but smile at each of them. He had enjoyed playing Santa tremendously. But then a sobering thought washed over him.

With the kitten for Mr. Rockingham, he had fulfilled Edith's wish of those three gifts. That meant her next letter—if she even sent one—would likely be the last. There would be no more letters to Santa. No more letters exchanged between the two of them. The very thought of it made him feel sick to his stomach.

He had been so caught up in having fun and enjoying their letter exchanges and his conversations with Edith over Santa that he had entirely forgotten it would come to an end. He smoothed the letters, then nervously smoothed them again. In a few days, this might be all he had left of this special exchange with Edith. And, again, it would be his own fault for holding back.

But, he'd been impulsive once today, hadn't he? Could he do it again? With something where the stakes were higher? George watched the small kitten stalk around the study, where it settled itself down eventually in the small bed he had made it near the fireplace. It had certainly made itself at home here. Could...Edith?

The wind began to howl outside. The repairs Freddy had made assured him his home would remain snug and dry. If only he felt so assured about his future with Edith. Had he made a terrible mistake pretending to be Santa?

He could neither tell her that had been him, nor tell her how he loved her.

George put the letters back into their envelopes, and leaned his head into the palms of his hands. What he needed right now was a Christmas miracle of his own. One to loosen his tongue and tell Edith how he cared for her—before any more time passed.

Chapter 17

"I think he's going to fire someone," Susan announced in a loud whisper.

"Why do you think that?" Edith asked with a frown. "George wouldn't do something like that right before Christmas."

"He has been watching everyone very closely," Freddy said, "though I don't think the man would do it before Christmas. Maybe things are bad at the bank and he does have to let someone go." He looked worried at the idea.

Edith wasn't sure that a layoff was why George had been watching everyone. She sensed an air of anxiety about him, as if something were bothering him. She just didn't know what. Her lunch break over, she hurried past George's closed office soon, went back behind the teller's counter, and yawned. Then, she stifled a second one as someone walked into the bank lobby.

She had stayed up late last night trying to finish George's scarf. It was almost done, and it was, without a doubt, the most beautiful scarf she had ever made. She had tried a very complicated stitch, but it would make sure the scarf was both warm and attractive. It required more attention than a simple scarf would require, but George was worth it, and she hoped it would please him.

Edith had been so tired last night that she had nearly fallen asleep while writing the letter to Santa, thanking him for the gift he'd sent. Today had been so busy, she hadn't even had a moment to give it to George and hoped to hand it to him while she was leaving work that day.

Mr. Rockingham had been absolutely overjoyed with the kitten. Mrs. Hedder, Widow Larson, and Edith had not been able to stop cooing over the precious little ball of fluff. The kitten had been named Sherlock, after one of Mr. Rockingham's favorite book characters.

The little fellow had quite made itself at home already, though it seemed to know Mr. Rockingham was his new best friend because he had crawled upon his shoulder, turned around a few times, and then settled himself into the small space by Mr. Rockingham's neck and fell asleep.

Mr. Rockingham had wiped away a few tears and could not stop smiling and touching the kitten. That morning when she had left for work, Mr. Rockingham had it tucked in one hand as he walked through the parlor.

"It's the perfect gift," Mrs. Hedder had exclaimed.

Edith could not agree more. She wasn't sure how in the world Santa had managed to find a kitten this time of year, but it was the most wonderful gift. Widow Larson had given Mr. Rockingham a length of twine, and they had taken turns teasing the kitten with it, watching the wee thing bounce after it.

Whoever Santa was, he'd brought Edith so much joy this Christmas, she'd be eternally grateful to him.

Freddy came down the stairs, his arms full of ledgers, and he settled himself at the counter. He pushed his glasses up on his nose. "Edith, George wants to have a word with you."

Susan gasped loudly. "Is he letting you go? And two days before Christmas! What a beast!"

"Susan, he's not letting any of us go." Freddy gave her a firm look. "I don't know why you insist on acting that way. Has the man ever been anything but than kind or fair? Look! You're scaring Madge half to death, and you even had me concerned earlier, before I thought it over."

Edith glanced at Madge, who was old enough to retire. The woman was trembling at her counter.

With a shrug, Susan said, "He likes to watch everyone. Always keeping an eye out on everything he does," she said with a nod.

"He's the owner of the bank," Edith sighed. "What else would he be doing?"

"This is different," Susan insisted.

"Remember Sal?"

Freddy interrupted her. "Sal was stealing from the bank. Good riddance to him. George is fair, and he's not firing anyone. Stop trying to bring dramatics into the workplace," he scolded. "We don't need that, especially not right before Christmas."

"Well, I never," Susan sniffed and turned her back.

Edith climbed the stairs, grateful that Freddy had said what he did, but now she felt a niggle of doubt from Susan's words. She really didn't think George would be firing her, but why did he want to see her in the middle of the workday?

She felt in her pocket. No matter, it was a good opportunity for her to give him her letter. She would also ask if it would be possible to see him for a couple of moments tomorrow so that she could give him the gift she had made. Though, she wouldn't tell him that part. She wanted to keep the fact she'd made him something a surprise.

Edith knocked on the door, and when he called out, she pushed it open. George had an extremely worried look on his face, and for a moment her stomach turned uncomfortably. Was Susan right and she was about to be let go?

She walked in and sat when he motioned to the chair. "Are you all right?" Edith asked after a moment.

"Yes, yes, I'm fine," George said. "I just have been wracking my brain all afternoon, all week, and all month trying to find the perfect gift for someone, and here we are two days before Christmas, and if I don't find it today, I won't be able to find it at all."

Edith sat back in her chair. It was hard for her to stop the smirk on her face. "Is that why you've been sulking about downstairs?"

"I've not been sulking," he retorted, crossing his arms and leaning back. "I've been observing. Making sure that I wasn't needed. And," he added, "hoping that something someone might say or do would jostle an idea into my mind."

"I see," Edith answered. "And did it?"

"No, it did not. Now, let's change the subject. Tell me," he said. "Did Santa come through on that third gift?"

"He did indeed," she answered. "George, I still can hardly believe what has happened. And it's the most wonderful gift. You'll never guess what it was."

"Then you'd better tell me," George said.

"A kitten!" Edith exclaimed.

"At this time of year?" George looked as stunned as she had been.

"Yes, indeed. It's the most wonderful thing. A darling little fluffy, adorable gray kitten. Mr. Rockingham is overcome with happiness." She produced the letter she'd written from her pocket. "May I trouble you to deliver one more letter for Santa? Do you mind?"

"Not at all," George said. "I'm happy to deliver it."

"Thank you," Edith said and stood. "I'd love to stay and chat, try to tease out from you who Santa is and who you are desperate to find a gift for, but it is still very busy downstairs, and I don't want the others to think I'm abandoning them."

"Who would think that?" George asked. "You'd never do such a thing."

Edith groaned. "Susan Cooper has got everyone on edge, saying that you're going to be letting someone go because of how you've been watching us all."

George stared at her in shock, and his mouth opened and closed a few times before he sputtered, "I would never do that. Especially not at Christmastime! The only reason I have ever let someone go was if their job performance was seriously lacking or they were stealing from the bank."

"That's what Freddy said," Edith nodded, "but you know how some people are. They like to stir up trouble as they go to make their days more enjoyable."

He nodded. "Yes, I do."

She was half out the door when he called out, "Edith?" She paused and turned back. "Could we meet up for just a couple of minutes tomorrow? The bakery will be open.

Perhaps we could go there again? There's something I want to tell you."

The look on his face was a pinched one. A cross between concern and fear. It wasn't something that Edith could ever recall seeing before. She wondered if George was even aware of how much emotion he was showing right now. Usually, he was quite composed.

The idea sounded perfect to Edith, even if a tiny twinge of worry over what he wanted to say spun through her. She'd wanted to see him tomorrow, anyway. If they met up, then she'd be able to give him the scarf that she had knitted.

She nodded, and was relieved to see his expression ease slightly. "What time? The bank is closed, and I have no plans."

"What about lunchtime?" George asked. "I'll buy us something to eat?"

"I'll meet you there," Edith promised, and hurried back downstairs.

The lobby was empty of customers, but Freddy, Madge, and Susan were staring at her. Each with a different expression. Edith laughed and shook her head. "I still have a job."

"Told you," Freddy said.

There was a large woosh of relief from Madge, but Susan just sniffed.

Edith settled back at her station, but let her thoughts drift back to George. She wondered what it was he wanted to talk with her about. The look on his face had been so strange, it seemed to her it must be important. Perhaps it would be a continuation of the conversation he had started a few days ago?

Edith couldn't lie to herself. She hoped he was going to tell her he still cared for her. That was the only thing she wanted this year for Christmas. But how could she confess that to anyone? Even Mrs. Hedder, who knew many of her secrets, had no idea that was her secret longing.

Still, the desire had nearly burst out of her chest. It was getting harder and harder to pretend she was fine with friendship, and nothing more. It wasn't that she was growing older and worried about her future. What worried her was the fact that George was such a fine man that, surely at any point, he'd announce he had plans to marry.

To her great shame, last night she'd been so overcome with exhaustion and tears as she realized this would be her last chance to send a letter to Santa. Reluctantly, she had given in and answered the question that he had asked so often. What would he think of that? And how in the world would Santa be able to give her the thing that she wanted most?

George.

Chapter 18

Two days. It was two days until Christmas. Edith hadn't let slip once what she wanted. He couldn't just get her an ordinary gift. None would do. Nothing was worthy of her. He'd taken to browsing the small collection of jewelry in town, imagining what it might be like to give her such a thing.

There had been whispers, as soon as he had, and he'd turned away, a lie fast on his lips: "Thank you, but I don't see anything my mother would care for."

George dropped his head into his hands. How often as of late had he done that gesture? Far too many times to count. Hopelessness filled him. And fear. Tomorrow, he was going to tell Edith. Tell her he cared for her. Loved her. He had no idea of her response. But, he was going to do it anyway.

He slumped down into his desk chair. The letter Edith had given him would be the last. He would miss their exchanges. Her radiant smile as she told about each gift Santa had given. Of course, there was no need to mail it. He'd read it, savor it, and—the letter!

George sat up so suddenly his neck jolted, sending a shooting pain through him. He rubbed it for a moment, then eagerly opened the letter Edith had left. Perhaps she'd mentioned what she wanted, at last.

This letter was longer than the one before, and he forced himself to read slowly. To cherish each word.

Dear Santa,

I want to thank you for each of the gifts you have given my friends. Their joy and happiness has added to my own this year. What had started as a bleak and painful season turned into one of miracles.

There is no doubt in my mind that each of them feels the same, especially Mr. Rockingham. He could hardly believe he was the recipient of such an adorable and loving little creature.

The kitten took to him as if he'd always known him. It's obvious they will be both the best of friends, and the companion that each needs. I don't know how you knew what to find him—or even where you did find such a thing this time of year—but thank you, Santa.

I hope that in the remaining days of this season, you are surrounded by all that you have need of, and all that you want. You are deserving of no less.

Santa, you've asked me several times what I want. I almost don't even dare tell you. It's too great. I don't dare hope for this, as miraculous as it would be, but my heart is so heavy with longing, and it aches, and tears come to me too often now, I have to tell someone.

George swallowed hard. There was a lump in his throat, and he could hear Edith's desperate words. What was paining her so much, that she wanted so very dearly, and held out no hope for? He refocused on the letter.

I am in love with someone.

There it was. He knew it. How could she not be? George set the letter down as tears blurred his vision and burned his eyes. He drew in a shuddering breath. Better to know, he told himself, and brushed away the moisture. Who was it?

I've been in love with George for years.

His heart suddenly pounded. Him! He was George! Wasn't he? He hoped he was the George she spoke of.

At one time, I thought that we would be together. That perhaps he felt the same. It's so hard to tell with him. George tends to hold his emotions tightly. To pull back and keep himself from some of the things that I think would make him happy.

George relaxed. It was him. He *was* the George she was in love with.

Santa, oh, dear, dear Santa, if you can help, please bring George the kind of life that he deserves. One filled with joys and happiness, someone to keep him company and be by his side. Even if that person isn't me, and even if my heart would shatter into a thousand pieces when the church bells rang for him, at least I'd know he'd be taken care of. That's all I want, Santa, for George to feel love.

Merry Christmas to you. There are no words to express all I hold in my heart for your kindness.

Yours,

Edith

The letter fell from George's stunned fingers, and floated gently to his desk. He stared at it in shock. After all this time, the thing she wanted, it wasn't even a wish for herself. It was a wish for him. Because she loved him.

Edith loved *him*.

Chapter 19

"Safe travels!" Edith cried after the stagecoach as it shuddered and flew down the street, picking up speed. She waved her handkerchief to the distant speck which she knew was Mrs. Hedder, and even though it was incredibly cold, the warmth in her heart contented her.

Christmas Eve was upon them. Mrs. Hedder had baked and cooked up a storm the last few days, and Edith and Widow Larson had helped. There was enough food for a week, perhaps, and then some. The boarding house owner had been almost afraid to leave her boarders, and Edith wondered if they'd have to put her onto the stage themselves.

Luckily, she'd gone, though she shouted out suggestions for them to care for themselves until her voice was so faint, they couldn't hear her.

"Goodness, thought she'd stay behind," Mr. Rockingham said. "Couldn't have that. Her son needs her." He glanced toward the boarding house. "And Sherlock needs me. We're going to have some warm milk together. See you ladies later."

"What are you going to do now?" Widow Larson asked as she pulled her shawl around her.

"I'm meeting a friend at the bakery so that I can give him my Christmas gift," Edith said, holding up the small parcel she held. "What of you?"

"A walk through town," Widow Larson said, "so that everyone can admire my shawl. See you soon, dear."

Edith waved, and set off toward the bakery. She hugged the package to herself, and hoped George would like the scarf. Oh yes, of course he'd say thank you, be polite. He'd like it. But she wanted him to like it. To really, really like it. To realize how much love was in it.

Her cheeks colored. What a silly thought. But her head had been full of that for some reason, ever since that moment in the bank. She just hoped that she wouldn't be terribly disappointed if what he wanted to tell her turned out to be something else.

Like he had his eye on someone else.

Edith closed her eyes for a moment, and then took a deep breath before she pushed on the bakery door. A quick glance showed she was there first. But before she could step forward more than twice, the door opened again, and George stood there, panting.

"I tried to run to hold the door for you," he explained. "But you were too quick."

She laughed. "Thank you, anyway," she told him.

"You here for lunch? We've a limited menu," the baker's wife apologized. "It being Christmas Eve. I have vegetable soup and crusty bread, and an assortment of pies."

"Then that's what we will have," George said. "And something warm to drink? My fingers are near frozen through."

Edith nodded in agreement, and followed George to the table by the window they'd occupied last time. They'd only just sat when the soup, bread and butter, and steaming tea and cider was set before them, along with two slices of pie, one apple and one cherry.

George pushed the cherry toward Edith with a wink, and she happily accepted it.

"Thank you for the lunch invitation," she said.

He seemed to squirm. "I just hope we are still friends after you hear what I have to say," he admitted.

Edith frowned. "Why wouldn't we be?" She set her bundle with his gift into her lap, and picked up her spoon.

"Well, you see..." George was quiet, broke off a piece of bread, then said, "Do you remember that time your locket went missing?"

"Yes, I do," she said. Her hand went to her neck as she remembered. The locket had been given to her by her grandmother. She still wore it, just not every day. "The clasp had broken," she recalled.

"And I found it, and took it to mend. I just didn't tell you, because I wanted it to be a surprise," Goerge said. "It's like that."

She shook her head. "I don't think I'm missing anything."

"No, I mean, perhaps I've meddled. But it was for good reason. And there's something else I have to tell you." George's voice was speeding up, and the piece of bread he was plucking in his nervousness was turning into crumbs. "But if I tell you one and don't have a chance to tell you the other..."

He stopped then, glanced down at the pile of crumbs before him, and shoved a bite into his mouth, effectively silencing himself.

Edith raised her brows. "Is that so? You'd best tell me then, before you ruin all the bread or work yourself into a mess."

He took a deep breath, and Edith watched him closely. "Promise you'll let me talk? Won't interrupt?" he asked. "Let me get through all of it before you either slap me or scold me or..."

When he stopped, she nodded. "I promise."

George took another deep breath. "I've been wanting to tell you. Trying to tell you. For years. But the words always jam in my throat. They get stuck. And I can't get them out."

He looked at her and didn't say anything else. Edith set her spoon down and prompted, "What words?"

George's eyes were filled with fear. It made her nervous. Edith took a sip of her tea, hoping it would hide her trembling fingers.

"That I like you," he whispered. "That I love you."

Edith sucked in a sharp breath. Had he just said...

"That I've wasted time," he continued. "Always let my fears get in the way."

He was quiet again, then shoved another bite of bread in his mouth, followed by one of soup. He stared at her.

"I'm not sure if I'm allowed to talk," Edith teased. "But so far, I don't mind what you've said." Her cheeks felt warm. "I've liked it, honestly."

"But that's the problem," George said quietly, and stirred his spoon around and around in the bowl. "Now you're going to think I'm not genuine."

"Why is that?" Edith asked.

"Because I found your letter. And I read it," George said.

"My letter?" Edith's heart sped up. "Maybe you'd best explain. I'll be quiet again."

George nodded. "When you went to mail the letters. I found yours, the first one, to Santa. I didn't mean to read it, but I wanted to know what you wanted for Christmas. I wanted to get you something special. Something to make you smile."

He frowned and shrugged. "But you didn't ask for anything for yourself. You asked for others. And when I bought those stage tickets, all at once I understood why you did what you had."

George shook his head slowly, and pressed a hand to his chest. "What I felt buying those tickets made me feel good. But later, when you told me more about Mrs. Hedder, and then later the Widow Larson, and Mr. Rockingham...how their lives had been so difficult. How something so small—to me—made such a change in their lives," he leaned forward, and said, "I understood. I thought my heart would burst. I was helping. Making a difference. And getting to do it all without worry someone would think I was doing it to look good."

George leaned back in his chair. "That might not make sense. None of it."

"It does," Edith said softly. "So, then, you were Santa. And kept it from me."

His face was one of misery. "Not to hurt you," he said softly. "Never that, Edith. I promise you."

She was quiet for a long moment. "I know," she said.

"You ended up giving me what I wanted most for Christmas," he said, shaking his head. "What you asked Santa for, you ended up giving me, by letting me bring joy to others, joy that ended up filling my own empty, aching soul."

Edith was still. There were too many thoughts in her mind right now, but she was choosing to focus on the one—George loved her.

"Don't be angry at me," George pleaded. He reached over and took her hands in his. "And please don't think that my affection toward you is anything but the truth."

Her eyes met his, and time seemed to still. Now it was time for her to say what she'd come to say.

Chapter 20

Edith gently pulled her hands back, and George let her. His heart sank. Then, he felt surprise, as she reached into her lap and produced a bundle he hadn't noticed.

"This is for you," Edith told him. "But if you open it, it comes with a condition."

George took the bundle from her, and turned it over. It didn't weigh much physically, but he could feel the weight in her words. There was a serious look on her face. He wanted to ask her what she thought about what he'd said, but stopped himself. Maybe this was her answer.

"What's the condition?" he asked instead.

Edith's lips twitched, and a small smile appeared. "If you open it, it also means you will take me on a date. One that will likely end in a kiss. And—"

George ripped open the paper. He wasn't about to give Edith a chance to change her mind. A soft scarf, a beautiful mossy green, fell into his hands. He recognized the color, and his pulse sped up. "This was for me?" he asked in wonder.

She nodded. "Yes."

He looked it over carefully. "I've never seen such fine work," he told her truthfully, and then wrapped it around his neck. "How does it look?"

"It looks perfect," she said.

George touched the softness around his neck. It didn't matter to him they were indoors. He'd never take it off, if he could help it.

"I had no idea this was for me," he said.

"I'm glad you liked this color," Edith said. "I wasn't sure which to choose."

"It's my favorite color," George said. "Do you know why?" When she shook her head, he reached for her hand again. "That was the color dress you were wearing the first time we met."

Edith's face turned a bright red, and George couldn't help but grin a little shyly. "Does this all mean that you forgive me?" he asked.

"There's nothing to forgive," Edith said. "You brought joy and happiness to so many. You've finally told me how you feel about me."

"I just wish I hadn't waited so long," he told her. "I've wasted too much time."

Edith dabbed at her lips, and pushed her empty pie plate away. "Then we have a lot to make up for."

George jumped up and held the door for her as they walked outside. Snowflakes lazily drifted down, the tiny ice crystals stinging his cheeks and nose, but he didn't care. Edith's hand was tight in his. Suddenly, he stopped, and faced her.

"Is anything wrong?" Edith asked.

"I don't want to wait any longer," George said. "I know that I love you. I know that you love me."

He dropped to one knee. "What do you say we go do something crazy and impulsive?"

Edith pulled him up, leaned in, and kissed George before he could realize what she was doing. "I think it's a wonderful idea," she told him as she stepped back.

George couldn't stop the silly grin on his face. "There's one thing we have to do," he said, and led her to a small brick store on the corner of the street.

Inside, the store owner, a man in a well-tailored suit, was just turning over the sign to Closed, but stopped when he saw them approach. "May I help you with something?" he asked.

"Yes," George said. "Let me see your rings. Edith has agreed to make me the happiest man alive."

As they left a short time later, Edith's hand still in his and a simple ring adorning her hand, George kept stealing glances at her.

They stopped, and Edith stepped close, adjusting the scarf around his neck again. She was so near, he could smell the honeysuckle-scented soap she'd bathed with. This moment, her so close, was all he'd dreamed of, and more, now that she was promised to be his.

"Thank you," George said, and took up her hand again.

"And thank you," she whispered, "Santa."

"Are you sure?" George asked, nervously. "I mean—"

"I won't change my mind," Edith laughed. "So you'd better not be trying to get out of it."

"I'm not," he answered with a grin. "Just making sure it's real."

"It's real," she told him, and then gestured around them, "as real as snow, and the sunshine, and Christmas, and Santa."

"I liked being Santa," he mused as they set off again down the street. "Let's do it again next year. Mr. and Mrs. Claus."

"I love that idea," Edith agreed, and then she stole a sideways glance at him. "Almost as much as I love you."

Epilogue

Eleven months later

"I've got the letters," George said, setting them on the table in front of Edith. He stopped and scratched the black cat's head as it tangled against his legs.

She looked at the pile before her. "There are almost three dozen," she said, shaking her head. "I thought there would be more."

Two months prior, she and George had spent a while forming a plan with Louise and Jake to create a special mailbox to hold letters to Santa that community members would write.

Volunteers from the local church and business owners each agreed to fulfill a number of the requests. Edith had anticipated a much higher number than simply three dozen.

"There might be a few others that find their way to us," George said. "But let's see what these are." He opened a letter. "This one is from a grandmother. She's raising her grandchildren, and they need something special to happen this year."

Edith nodded, and then held up another letter. "This one is from a young boy who wants to buy his mother a gift."

"Let's sort, and then distribute the letters," George said as the housekeeper bustled around in the kitchen.

An hour later, there were a half dozen letters that Edith and George decided they wanted to fulfill, and they'd separated the rest to go to the other volunteers.

"It's a lovely tradition we have started," Edith said as she wrapped her shawl around her and they stepped out onto the porch.

"A needed one," George said grimly. "But I feel fortunate so many are helping us now."

"I love playing Mrs. Santa," Edith said happily as they strode down the street toward the church, where the first packet of letters would be dropped off.

"You'd best make sure you don't forget to write your own letter to Santa," George said. "He needs to know what you want for Christmas."

Edith laughed, and wrapped her arm through his. "I already have what I want. You!"

"Yes, but I want to get you something," George answered. "And you don't make it easy to guess what."

She laughed again, and teased, "Don't worry, you've time to figure something out."

George scowled. "You have something in mind, but won't tell me," he said. "I can sense it."

With a shrug, Edith raised her brows. "I really don't know what you mean," she said.

"This is what got us into this whole situation," George grumbled. Then he grinned at her. "Luckily."

Edith didn't answer. She was having too much fun teasing George. He was right, though. Her letter to Santa, and his persistence in desiring to know what gift she wanted, did lead to this—an outcome she'd hardly dared dream of.

Two months after Christmas Eve, they had married. Edith still worked at the bank; she enjoyed it too much to stop. It also brought in a little extra income that they called the Christmas fund. It was used to surprise others with, as they played Santa.

Though only a select few knew who the mysterious benefactors would be for those in Richmond who needed a Christmas miracle, Edith had a feeling their new tradition would continue to grow and expand. Perhaps even into other towns. Louise's sister, Mathilda, was very interested in doing something like that herself.

A sharp gust of wind blew, knocking Edith's hat askew and making George's scarf come loose. She stopped, readjusted it, and pecked him on the lips. "Would you like a new scarf for Christmas?" she asked.

"This will always be my favorite," he answered. "Just as you will be."

"But what would you like for Christmas?" she asked as they resumed their walk.

"I'll tell you," George said, "but it comes with a condition." As she looked at him, he grinned. "You have to tell me what you want."

Edith laughed, and smacked at him. "Oh you!" At his hopeful look, she grinned. "Fine. Write Santa. Perhaps you'll get an answer."

"I will," he promised. "I'm a believer in Christmas miracles and letters to Santa."

"Me too," Edith agreed. "After all, I got all I wanted, thanks to him."

George didn't answer, just grinned at her and took her hand. Edith returned his smile, and they quietly walked home together, just as it was always been meant to be.

Note from Author

Thank you for taking the time to read Letters to Santa! Could I ask for one small favor? Reviews like yours on Amazon mean so much to me and help others to find my books! Even just a single line means a lot!

Also...

Want a FREE book?

Stop by my website to get your no strings attached **FREE book**. It's my gift to you, as a thank you for reading this one.

www.sarahlambbooks.com

Wait...there's more!

If you enjoyed this story, you might also like to meet Louise and hear how she escaped on and from the Titanic. Here's her story.

Louise

The night before her wedding and honeymoon on *Titanic's* maiden voyage, Louise discovers the man she was to marry is a hardened criminal. Desperate to escape and protect her younger sister, she does the only thing she can think of to hide—become a mail order bride and mother to two young children. Louise knows nothing of mothering or managing a home, and it's sure to be the perfect cover.

But when Louise arrives at her destination, she's surprised to learn she's not the only one with a secret. With peril surrounding them, will the man she's supposed to marry help once he discovers her past and the danger she's brought to his quiet life? Or will the secrets from his past return to hurt them both?

https://www.amazon.com/Louise-Rescue-Mail-Order -Brides-ebook/dp/B0BJ9NXZWF

***

And, you also might want to meet Mathilda, Louise's sister who escaped on the Titanic with her.

Mathilda

The last thing Mathilda thought she'd be doing was boarding the *Titanic* to escape the danger hot on her heels. With knowledge of important papers that could get her killed and a wad of money, she's trying to get as far away as she can with her older sister.

Fleeing for her life, she becomes a mail order bride. However, Mathilda discovers she might not be able to keep her past a secret. The man she's supposed to marry is a policeman, with a sixth sense she's hiding something. He's also the kindest man she's ever met, and she's quickly falling in love with him.

By the time Mathilda decides to confess the truth and hope for the best, as well as his love in return, it may be too late, and lives may be lost.

https://www.amazon.com/Mathilda-Rescue-Mail-Order-Brides-ebook/dp/B0BJ9PKMHQ

About the Author

Sarah writes captivating characters and clean romance that's anything BUT boring! From heartbreaking moments to heartwarming tales, get swept away in either historical or small town romance that pulls you in until the last page.

Nestled in the Blue Ridge Mountains of Virginia where she's married to her Texan husband, you'll find Sarah creating her next book, homeschooling her two boys, or volunteering in her community.

There are other great books in this series as well!

Find all the Western Christmas Magic books on Amazon!

https://www.amazon.com/dp/B0DC5L6FZG

***

Want more of Sarah's books? She writes for children and adults! Find them all on Amazon!

https://www.amazon.com/stores/Sarah-Lamb/author/B098H3SGLK